"There's something I need to do."

Rose was closer still. There were only centimeters separating them, and suddenly the distance was nothing at all.

She was kissing him. Her lips were pressed against his, slightly parted; they were warm and soft, softer than he'd imagined.

She tasted of strawberries.

That was unexpected.

Everything was unexpected but not unpleasant.

Mitch could feel his body responding. His reaction was immediate, and while it was completely understandable it was also completely out of his control.

He hadn't been a monk since Cara died, but it had been months since he'd been with a woman. It wasn't easy on the station. He didn't get a lot of time or opportunity, and here was Rose presenting him with opportunity. He wasn't about to argue.

But he had his own idea of how this was going to go.

He took control, deepening the kiss. His tongue parted her lips and her mo as she melted under his.

Dear Reader,

I'm so pleased to finally give you Rose's story, the third in my Tempted & Tamed miniseries. Many of you wrote to me after reading the first two books asking me to write Rose's story. It was always my intention to do that, although it has taken a little longer than I planned! But I think it's worked out well, as Rose had plenty of obstacles to overcome and she needed some time before she was ready to fall in love. I also needed time to find her the perfect man, and I hope I have done that with Mitch.

Rose is the youngest of the three Anderson sisters—Scarlett, Ruby and Rose—and the last one to find her happily-ever-after. If you missed the first two books, you can read about Scarlett and Ruby in *A Doctor by Day…* and *Tamed by the Renegade*.

If you have a chance to read all three books, I'd love to know if you've enjoyed them. Did you have a favorite? Drop me a line at emilyforbes@internode.on.net.

Until then, happy reading,

Emily

A MOTHER TO
MAKE A FAMILY

———

EMILY FORBES

HARLEQUIN® MEDICAL ROMANCE™

Recycling programs for this product may not exist in your area.

ISBN-13: 978-0-373-21522-5

A Mother to Make a Family

First North American Publication 2017

Copyright © 2017 by Emily Forbes

Printed in U.S.A.

Books by Emily Forbes

Harlequin Medical Romance

The Christmas Swap
Waking Up to Dr. Gorgeous

The Hollywood Hills Clinic
Falling for the Single Dad

Tempted & Tamed
A Doctor by Day…
Tamed by the Renegade

His Little Christmas Miracle
A Love Against All Odds

Visit the Author Profile page
at Harlequin.com for more titles.

For everyone who asked me for Rose's story;
thank you for your patience and I really hope
you enjoy this,

Emily

**Praise for
Emily Forbes**

"Have your tissues ready because you are gonna
need them…it's that good! Prepare to be hooked
on Medical Romance and Emily Forbes!"

—*Goodreads* on
A Love Against All Odds

CHAPTER ONE

A SCREAM SPLIT the air, cleaving through the thick muggy silence that suffocated the land.

Mitch recognised the sound and it sent a shiver of fear down his spine.

The hairs on the back of his neck rose up and the wrench fell from his hand as he sprinted from the shed.

He was halfway to the horse yards before the scream ended and the silence that followed stabbed at his heart. He'd never known silence to be so terrifying. It was ominous. After thirty-nine years he knew trouble when he heard it.

The sound of his boots as they slapped the dirt echoed across the ground and the pounding of his feet imitated the pounding of his heart, which had lodged somewhere in his throat. He listened for more noise, another sound, anything, as he ran. Anything would be better than the oppressive silence.

Time stood still. Red dust flew from under

his boots but it might as well have been quick-sand. The horse yards weren't getting any closer.

He rounded the corner of the staff quarters and almost collided with his six-year-old son.

'Dad, Dad, come quick! It's Lila.' Jed grabbed Mitch's hand but Mitch didn't slow his pace and his hand pulled out of his son's grasp. He still didn't stop. He'd make better time alone. He kept running, knowing Jed would follow.

He had to get to Lila. He had to get to his daughter.

He skidded into the horse yards and felt Jed come to a stop beside him. He scanned the enclosures, searching for his two other children.

Charlie was standing still. He was holding Ruff, their Australian terrier, in his arms. The little dog was squirming and wriggling, desperate to get down. Ruff wasn't supposed to be anywhere near the horse yards but Mitch didn't have time to think about that now.

His daughter lay flat on her back on the hard, red ground. Her face was ashen and she lay as still as a corpse, her eyes open. His heart was lodged firmly in his throat now and he fought to breathe. The air was thick and muggy, choking him as he tried to force it into his lungs. He'd already lost one daughter. He couldn't lose Lila too. His children were all he had left.

And then he saw her chest move. Rising and falling as she breathed.

She was alive.

The lump in his throat dislodged and he sucked in a breath.

Ginny was kneeling over her and Mitch crouched in the dirt beside her.

'Lila!'

He wanted to gather her into his arms, to pick her up and carry her away, but he didn't dare move her. He knew it wasn't safe.

His daughter's lips were parted, her eyes huge and dark in her pale face. They brimmed with tears and her bottom lip wobbled.

'It hurts.'

Mitch could hear the catch in her voice and it was almost more than he could bear. 'Where?'

'My back.'

Shit.

'You haven't moved her, have you?' he asked Ginny. He hadn't acknowledged the governess until now. He'd been far too intent on Lila.

'No.' Ginny shook her head. 'She landed like this.'

The ground was as hard as concrete. They'd had no rain in this distant corner of Queensland for three years, even the river was dry. The station was relying on water from the artesian basin for the cattle, there was nothing spare to soften the ground or water the gardens. Who knew what injuries Lila might have sustained? What damage had been done?

Mitch slipped his fingers into Lila's palm. 'Can you squeeze my hand?'

He relaxed ever so slightly as he felt the re-assuring squeeze.

'Don't move your legs,' he told her, 'but see if you can wriggle your toes.'

Lila was wearing elastic-sided riding boots. He couldn't see if she was moving her toes but she winced.

'Could you do it?' he asked.

'Yes. But it hurt.'

That was a good sign, Mitch thought. Not that he wanted his daughter to be in pain but pain was often absent in serious spinal injuries. 'I know, sweetie, you're being very brave.'

Tears spilled from Lila's lashes onto her cheeks.

Mitch wiped the tears from her face. 'It'll be all right, Lila.'

He turned and spoke to Ginny. 'What happened?' It didn't really matter what had happened, what mattered was getting some help, but he had to know. He had to make some sense of the situation.

'Ruff got loose. He spooked Fudge and she threw Lila off,' Ginny explained. 'I'm sorry. It all happened so quickly, there was nothing I could do.'

Ginny sounded upset but Mitch didn't doubt her recounting of the incident.

He glanced over to where his stockman was standing with Lila's horse's reins firmly in his hands. Both Jimmy and the horse were standing quietly against the railing of the yard. Jimmy was keeping the horse as far away from Charlie and the dog as he could without going out of sight. Mitch knew that Jimmy would have calmed the horse and then stayed in the vicinity in case Mitch needed him. Seeing Jimmy settled his nerves to some degree. Despite his physical disability Jimmy was the best horse handler Mitch had ever seen and he knew that something must have happened that had been out of his control. Fudge had a placid temperament normally but for some reason she hated the little dog with a passion and Ruff reciprocated her feelings and delighted in nipping at her rear hooves. Jimmy never would have let the little dog within cooee of the horse.

But Mitch didn't have time to think about the dog or the horse and he didn't have time for re-criminations either. Ginny had been the governess on the station for the past twelve months; she was responsible and level-headed, she'd grown up on cattle stations and knew her way around horses. Mitch knew she had the best interests of his children at heart—that was why he'd hired her. Ginny was close to tears and Mitch needed her to stay composed—he needed her to look after the boys. Neither Ginny nor Jimmy would have made a deliberate error. It sounded like an accident and he wasn't looking for anyone to blame. He knew from past experience that it made no difference to the outcome. What was done was done, and his priority now was Lila.

Thankfully she'd been wearing her helmet. Thank goodness she'd had some protection. He didn't remove it. He couldn't risk the movement. Not until her injuries had been assessed. He knew what to do but she needed more attention than he was able to give her and somehow, when the situation was personal, it became harder to remain objective. He didn't want to do the wrong thing. And that was the trouble—he didn't trust his own judgement any more. Lila needed medical attention, but they were in Outback Queensland, hundreds of kilometres and a five-hour drive from the nearest hospital.

'Go to the house,' he instructed Ginny. 'Call the flying doctor on the satellite phone and bring it back to me along with the medical chest.'

She stood up and Mitch noticed that her knees were shaking, her hands too, and her face was ashen. Everyone was on edge. 'Take the dog,' he called after her as she hurried away. Ginny came back and took Ruff from Charlie's arms. 'And make sure he's tied up.'

He turned back to his daughter. 'Do you know what day it is, Lila?' he asked.

'Wednesday,' she replied, and Mitch breathed a sigh of relief.

'Do you know what happened?'

'I came off Fudge.'

As far as assessments for concussion went it was as basic as they came but hearing the correct responses was a positive sign. Her eyes were open, she wasn't confused and she could move independently even if it hurt. Fourteen points out of a possible fifteen on the Glasgow coma scale, Mitch thought automatically, although that was only part of the story.

He sat in the dirt and held Lila's hand as he waited for Ginny to return. Waiting was the hardest thing. He was useless until he had the medical chest and even that wouldn't be enough. He was pretty certain that Lila had sustained fractures and there was the risk that she had also suffered internal injuries but he didn't want to start an assessment. He didn't want to be the one to cause her pain. He'd wait for the medical chest, at least then he'd be able to check her blood pressure and get a bit of an indication as to what they were dealing with but he was convinced she would have to be evacuated. They needed the flying doctor.

He kept talking. Soft, nothing words, just sounds really, letting her know he was there, that he wasn't going to leave her.

Her eyes fluttered closed and he fought back another wave of panic while he reminded himself that she didn't seem concussed. She seemed alert enough, even if she was in pain.

'Is she going to be okay, Dad?'

Jed stood beside him and Mitch noticed that he had his arm wrapped around his little brother, comforting him. Mitch should be doing that but he found himself stretched to the limit, as had been the case so often in the past two years. There just wasn't enough of him to go around.

'She'll be fine,' he replied. He had no other answer. He didn't want to lie but he had to believe she would be okay. He had to believe his own words.

'You can fix her, can't you, Dad?'

'I'm going to need some help, Jed, but the flying doctor will be here soon. Why don't you and Charlie go down to the kitchen for smoko?'

He hadn't heard the bell but it must be nearly time for morning tea. The station staff would all converge on the kitchen and a drink and a piece of cake would keep the boys occupied.

Ginny returned on one of the quad bikes. She

had the medical chest strapped to the back of the bike and a blanket thrown over her lap. She carried the medical chest over and put it down beside Mitch before draping the blanket over Lila. Mitch hadn't thought of the blanket, the temperature was nudging thirty-four degrees Celsius, but if Lila went into shock he might need it.

'The plane is on its way and the base is holding for you,' Ginny said as she handed him the satellite phone.

Mitch knew that depending on where the plane was coming from it could take an hour to reach them. He took the phone as he instructed Ginny to get his head stockman and pilot to prepare the runway for the plane.

He spoke to the doctor at the Broken Hill base and relayed the information he had while he opened the medical chest and found the few things he needed. He checked her blood pressure, kept her warm and gave her some pain relief and then he waited.

And waited.

Time stood still as his daughter lay in the dirt, in pain.

Lila looked so like her mother that Mitch's heart ached every time he looked at her. Dark hair, dark eyes. All three of the children had his dark eyes but the boys were much more like him. They had the same white blond hair he'd had as a child. His hair had darkened with age and had even gone a little grey with stress.

He'd been trying his best not to let his feelings show over the past two years. He didn't want the children to grow up sensing his pain. His loss. It was their loss too but he knew they felt it differently. They were so young, so much more resilient than he felt, but he'd vowed to do his best by them.

He'd become very good at disguising his feelings, an expert at pretending everything was okay. But he didn't know if he had the strength to get through another tragedy. Hopefully it wouldn't come to that, but if it did he'd have to find the reserves somewhere. The children were all he had and he was all they had.

He knew he had to keep his composure, had to stay calm, and he was grateful that no one else had been injured. He'd seen more than his fair share of injuries, and even a couple of fatalities, from accidents with horses. But being around horses was a way of life on the station and Mitch knew it was important that the children were familiar with them. Of course, he'd always insisted that they wear helmets when they were riding and fortunately that was a rule they'd never broken. Lila's accident could have been much worse; it wasn't as bad as it got but it was close.

In the distance he heard the sound of an engine. The familiar whine of the flying doctor plane. It was coming from the west and he looked at the sky, searching for a flash of silver and white. There. The plane was silhouetted against the endless, clear blue sky. He watched as it dropped lower, heading for the dirt landing strip behind the outbuildings, and waited again for the doc.

Darren, the head stockman, pulled up in a dusty four-wheel-drive and the doc and the flight nurse piled out. He recognised Doc Burton. Mitch reckoned he'd worked with all of the doctors over the years. He nodded in acknowledgement and then relayed what he knew of the events, what he'd given Lila for pain relief, and her medical history and then he stepped aside to let them examine his daughter. He wasn't one of them any more, he was just Lila's father.

Lila was alert and talking as they checked her pupils, got her to move her fingers and toes and gradually worked their way up her limbs. She seemed to be able to move her upper limbs reasonably comfortably but her legs were a different story. Doc Burton gently palpated Lila's neck before removing her helmet. He moved to her abdomen as the nurse retested her blood pressure.

Lila cried out in pain as the doc pressed on her pelvis and Mitch had to restrain himself from leaping in and stopping the examination right there. He couldn't stand to see Lila in more pain.

'Temp thirty-six point two degrees, pulse one hundred, respirations twenty-two, BP ninety on sixty, oxygen ninety-eight percent.' The flight nurse relayed Lila's vital statistics.

'Can you run five hundred millilitres of normal saline and draw up five milligrams of morphine? I want to give her a shot before we move her.' The doc finished speaking to the nurse before turning to Mitch.

'I agree with you,' he said, 'there's no apparent head injury and her spine seems okay but it looks like she has a fractured pelvis so we'll need to take her with us to the base.' Back to Broken Hill, to the hospital. 'I don't think she has major internal injuries, her observations are quite reasonable, which suggests that there's no excessive internal bleeding but I won't really know until we get her to Broken Hill for scans. She may need to go to Adelaide but you know the drill.'

The doc took the syringe from the nurse and injected the morphine into Lila's abdomen.

'This will sting a little, Lila, but it will work fast to take the pain away,' he told her.

Mitch knew the drill all too well. Doc Burton would take away the pain and then he'd take Lila. Mitch had known that would be the case. He'd known her injuries were too severe to be treated out here. He'd known she would need to go to hospital and he would follow. He hadn't set foot in a hospital for two years but that was all about to change. He'd known the day would come when he'd have to face up to the past and that day was now. He would have to cope, for Lila's sake.

He picked up Lila's hand, holding it, not sure whether he was comforting her or himself.

'All right, we need to get her in the plane.' Doc Burton looked at Mitch and Mitch knew his face would be pale under his tan. 'You're coming?'

Mitch nodded as the doc and the flight nurse wrapped a brace around Lila's pelvis and rolled her onto a spinal board. He'd managed to avoid the hospital for two years but deep down he'd wondered what it would take to get him back there. Now he knew. This was it.

Mitch looked at the length of the stretcher and then at the four-by-four utility parked nearby. The ground was dry, hard and corrugated, he didn't want to drive Lila over it to the airstrip.

'Can we carry her back to the plane?' he suggested. 'Three of us should manage it easy.'

Jimmy had taken the horse back to the stables, leaving just the three men and the flight nurse. Mitch put himself at the foot of the stretcher where he could keep an eye on his daughter. Doc Burton and Darren took one side each at the head and the flight nurse loaded the equipment back into the four-by-four and drove it back to the airstrip. The boys came running from the kitchen as the procession headed to the runway. Charlie tagged at Jed's heels, doing his best to keep up with his older brother.

Ginny fell into step beside Mitch. 'You're going with her.' Her words weren't a question. He nodded and Ginny took the boys' hands as they reached the airstrip, keeping them under control, one on each side of her. Thank goodness he had Ginny to help out. But not for much longer. Ginny was leaving soon, heading off to travel the world with her boyfriend. Mitch needed to do something about finding a replacement but that was a problem for another day. He had enough to worry about for the time being.

Once Lila was loaded onto the plane Mitch bent and kissed the tops of his sons' heads. 'Ginny will look after you,' he said. 'I'll be back as soon as I can.'

'Lila too?' Charlie asked. He adored his sister

and followed her around constantly. The boys would be lost without Lila. So would he. He couldn't imagine losing all the women in his family.

'Lila too,' Mitch replied, hoping he could keep his promise.

Shirley, the cook, had appeared from the kitchen and she pressed a paper bag into his hands. He knew the bag would contain food and although he couldn't imagine that he'd feel like eating he took the bag anyway, he knew it was her way of coping. He climbed into the plane, choosing a seat from where he could keep watch.

Lila was drowsy now, the pain relief was working, and as the engines started up her eyelids fluttered and closed.

Through the window Mitch watched the station fall away as the pilot lifted the plane into the air. Red dirt, chestnut cattle, the dry, stony creek, grey-green trees and the silver, corrugated-tin roofs of the buildings that glinted in the sunlight. He looked down onto Jed and Charlie as they stood at the edge of the runway and watched him leave.

He could see it all laid out before him, his entire life, and he wondered when it would get back to normal. Would it ever?

The past two years had been the most difficult of his life. How many more traumatic events could they be expected to endure?

The last time he had been in the flying doctor plane on his way to Broken Hill he'd been with his wife and unborn child.

He turned away from the window, his gaze seeking Lila. He was determined to come back with his daughter. He couldn't bear the thought of returning alone again.

CHAPTER TWO

ROSE'S RIGHT FOOT ACHED, complaining about being crammed into uncomfortable shoes. She should have worn socks, she thought, something that would cushion her misshapen foot from the unforgiving canvas of her sneakers, but socks had looked ugly so she'd gone without and now she was paying the price for her vanity.

She had to wear closed-toe shoes for work but she wished she could wear ballet flats, something prettier than canvas sneakers. Work dress rules allowed ballet flats but she couldn't wear them any more. They wouldn't stay on.

Rose undid the laces and slipped her shoe off. She hated these shoes, hated the fact that she couldn't wear anything pretty any more. She hadn't minded these shoes on occasion before, but *having* to wear them, or something similar, every day had certainly taken the gloss off. She was sick of the sight of them. And the feel.

Once upon a time appearances had been so

important to her but she was having to adjust her thinking on that. She was having to adjust her thinking on a lot of things.

Gone were the days of wearing her towering, strappy, glamorous shoes. She was prepared to admit that by the end of an evening out she had always been glad to remove them, they hadn't necessarily been made for comfort but they had been pretty. Now she had traded impractical, pretty and uncomfortable shoes for practical, *ugly* and uncomfortable. If she had to sacrifice comfort she wished she could at least look pretty.

Winter would be better, she thought. She could get a pair of flat boots. She'd tried wearing ankle boots but even in the air-conditioned hospital rooms her foot had got too hot and it had swelled up and ached even more.

She rubbed her foot on the back of her left calf, trying to get her circulation going. She knew she was supposed to be desensitising her foot by rubbing it regularly with different textures but she hated even looking at it let alone touching it. How ridiculous that toes that didn't exist any more could give her so much trouble.

She knew that her toes had had to be amputated. She knew there hadn't been a choice but that didn't mean she had to like it.

And now she knew all about phantom limb

pain. Thank goodness she wasn't missing an entire limb; she could only imagine how painful that would be.

She needed to remember to be grateful. Her psychologist had told her to keep a list of all the things she was grateful for and to recall it when she was feeling maudlin. She started to run through the list in her head as she continued to rub her foot.

She was alive. That was a big one. A good one to start the list.

From the outside she looked the same but Rose knew that looks could be deceptive. She was different on the inside and underneath, but she didn't have to show those parts of her to anyone. She could keep that hidden, which was exactly what she intended to do.

Two—she had finished her degree and was now a qualified teacher. But that was as far as she got running through her 'grateful' list before the door into the office she shared with two other teachers opened and her manager walked in. Rose quickly tucked her right foot under her desk, hiding it from view, and slid it into her sneaker.

Jayne was a tall woman, her grey hair closely cropped to her head, her frame athletic, a little masculine. She was hard muscle from all the running she did and there was nothing left to soften the edges. Rose hadn't known her long but she seemed to be constantly on the go, always training for a running event, a half-marathon or marathon. That was something else Rose wasn't able to do—run. She'd never imagined that losing three small toes would make such an impact. Her doctors had told her she would be able to run again but she wasn't sure about that yet.

'Rose, do you have time to see one more patient before you finish for the weekend?' Jayne asked.

Rose closed the browser on her laptop as she replied. 'Sure.' Despite the fact it was Friday night she had nothing she needed to rush home for. That wasn't unusual; her social life had taken a battering—spending months in hospital tended to do that—and her confidence had also suffered. She hadn't dated for two years and she wasn't sure she was ready for that to change. She had nothing in her life except for work, her mother, her sisters and her niece. But that was okay. That was enough to handle at the moment.

'The patient's name is Lila Reynolds, she's eight years old. Her parents haven't requested educational support but the social worker is advocating for it. She says Lila is very withdrawn.

She's from Outback Queensland and doesn't have any family support here in Adelaide.'

Rose remembered being eight years old. That was the year her father had died. The year she had gone from being his little princess and thinking the world was perfect to realising that it wasn't and that just because you wished something was so didn't make it real. It was one of life's lessons that she was relearning again at the age of twenty-three.

'No one?' she asked.

Jayne shook her head. 'The social worker has been leaving messages for her parents but is yet to speak to them. There's no file yet.'

Rose knew the files were often not much help anyway. The file the education system, and therefore the teaching staff, had access to was different from the case notes that the hospital staff—doctors, nurses, social workers, physios and the like—wrote in. The teachers weren't privy to all the private and sometimes confidential information about their young pupils but were given just the basic facts. Age, gender, and medical diagnosis were shared but only so that the teachers were aware of any impediments that would affect their learning. They were often given just enough information to put the children into the system but not enough to be useful—Rose could remember one of the other teachers telling her that when she'd first started this job.

'The social worker thinks it might be helpful to have one of us spend some time with Lila unofficially while she continues trying to speak to the parents,' Jayne said. 'She thought that if you had time you might have more luck with getting her to talk.'

In the six months since Rose had started working at the Royal Children's Hospital she knew she had garnered a reputation as someone who had a good rapport with the more reserved children. She'd always felt a connection with the quieter kids. She could empathise with their emotional scars and now, from more recent experience, with their physical scars as well.

'And if that doesn't work,' Jayne continued, 'then the consensus is that if you can give her something to occupy her time then she might at least get some benefit from that.'

'I'll see what I can do,' Rose replied. 'What are her injuries?'

'She was thrown from a horse and sustained pelvic fractures. She was transferred from Broken Hill to Adelaide and underwent surgery a week ago. Her pelvis was pinned but she is able to get out of bed and can now move around with the aid of a walking frame.'

'Okay.'

Rose stood as Jayne left the office. She reached up and ran her fingers along the spines of her selection of books that she'd stored on the shelves. Since starting this job she'd added to her collection of children's books and she chose a few now that she thought might be of interest to an eight-year-old. If Lila didn't want to talk perhaps Rose could read to her. If Lila had been rushed to Adelaide for emergency surgery she probably hadn't brought much with her. Reading might help to pass the time and also might prompt a conversation. It had worked in the past.

Rose tucked the well-worn volumes under her arm. She loved shopping in markets and second-hand stores, something her sister Ruby had fostered in her, but while Ruby had always bought clothes, Rose had spent her time searching through the old books. Scarlett, her eldest sister, had started reading to her after her dad had died. Escaping into a book had helped her to get over her grief but it had also fed her imagination. She liked drama, tales of princesses, weddings, romance and young love. She wished the real world was more like her literary world. She didn't choose to read stories about war or crime or misery. She chose books where the characters got to live happily ever after.

She tugged on the back of her right sneaker,

pulling it up over her heel to secure the shoe. God, she hated these shoes. If anything, her foot was even more uncomfortable now than before. She had thought these shoes would be okay but by the end of the day her feet ached and in reality these shoes probably didn't have enough support. She didn't think she was on her feet a lot but the hospital was big and there was a fair bit of walking just to get from the main entrance to the wards and to the classrooms. Which was good for her fitness but not so good for her feet.

The familiar smell of the hospital ward assailed her as she stepped out of the elevator by the orthopaedic wards. She didn't spend a lot of time on the wards, most of her time was spent in the classrooms, but the distinctive smell of the hospital was hard to ignore and hard to forget. She thought it was lodged in her subconscious, a lingering and not altogether pleasant after-effect of her time spent in ICU and the transplant ward.

She checked in with the charge nurse before heading into the four-bed ward to find Lila. Only two beds were occupied. It was mid-afternoon and Rose knew the ward had probably been full this morning but paediatric patients got discharged quickly and regularly, especially in the orthopaedic wards. There was a high turnover when patients could be sent home to be cared for by their parents.

Rose suspected that Lila would be in hospital for some time. It would be difficult to discharge her home to Outback Queensland if she needed rehabilitation for her injuries. Rose had learnt a lot in the past six months about a whole host of medical conditions. In fact, she'd learnt a lot in the eighteen months prior to that too but that had all been to do with her own experience.

A girl of about five years of age was in a bed to Rose's left and on the opposite side of the room, next to the window lay a girl who looked more likely to be Lila. Rose scanned the patient names above each bed just to be sure before she crossed the room.

'Lila?' she asked as she stopped beside the bed. She was a dark-haired, solemn-eyed little girl. Her skin was tanned and appeared healthy and brown against the white hospital sheets. She was thin but apart from that she looked too healthy for a hospital ward.

The little girl nodded.

'My name is Rose. I've brought you some books to pass the time. Do you like to read?'

Lila shook her head.

'Oh.' Rose put the books on the bedside cupboard but she refused to be deterred.

'What *do* you like to do?'

'Ride my horse.' There was no elaboration but at least she was talking.

'What about when it's raining?'

'It never rains.'

'Never?'

Her question was answered with another silent shake of her head.

'Oka-a-a-y…' Rose drew out the word as she thought about what to ask next. 'What about if it's too *hot* to go outside?'

'Then I like to draw.'

'What do you draw?' Rose asked as she looked around, expecting to see some drawings taped to the walls, but the walls were bare. 'Have you got any drawings?'

Lila nodded.

'Would you show me?' Rose asked.

Lila pulled a piece of paper from the bedside drawer and held it up. 'It's not very good 'cos I don't have any pencils.'

The paper was lined, Rose recognised it from the hospital case notes, but on it Lila had drawn a fabulous picture of a horse.

'Is this your horse?' Rose asked.

Lila nodded.

'What's her name?'

'Fudge.'

'That's an interesting name.'

'She's the same colour as caramel fudge,' Lila

explained, 'but it's hard to tell 'cos the nurses could only find a lead pencil.'

'Well, I think she's beautiful.'

Rose noticed that Lila's voice became a little more animated when she was talking about her horse. Maybe that was the secret to getting her to engage. But wasn't that the same with all children? You just needed to find something that they were interested in. Rose knew that if you did that it was often hard to stop them from sharing.

'Does she smell like caramel?'

'That's silly.' Lila couldn't hide her smile. 'Horses don't smell like caramel.'

'Well, what does she smell like?'

'She smells like a horse.' Lila giggled and her dark eyes sparkled, losing their serious intensity. She looked like an eight-year-old girl now and Rose had a moment of self-satisfaction that she'd been able to make this little girl laugh. That she had been able to make a connection, however small, gave her a sense of achievement. This was what she loved about teaching, establishing a connection with the children.

Lila's giggles continued and Rose knew she was intrigued, but before she could say anything further she became aware of someone on the periphery of her vision. Someone else waiting and watching as she listened to Lila's laughter.

She looked up to find a man standing in the doorway of the ward.

Possibly the most gorgeous man she had ever seen.

Tall, dark and handsome.

Her heart skipped a beat as she wondered who he was. A doctor she hadn't met yet? An orthopaedic surgeon? She was certain she'd never seen him before—his was not a face she would forget.

Rose ran her eyes over him. He would be a shade over six feet tall with a slim build but his shoulders and chest were broad, his arms were strong and muscular and his legs were long. He was casually dressed in jeans and a navy T-shirt, not the normal doctor-on-staff out-fit—no white surgical coat, no tell-tale stetho-scope—but Rose noted these things almost subconsciously as her gaze remained locked on his face. His very handsome face. It was tanned and he had a full head of thick, brown hair, cut short, with dark brown eyes to match. His jaw was triangular, darkened by a shadow of stubble, and he had a slight smile on his lips.

She bent her knees and her thighs tensed, ready to push her out of her chair, ready to cross the room and introduce herself to a handsome stranger. It was a reflex response, a reaction completely outside her conscious control, but before she could actually complete the movement the rest of her brain woke up and she realised what she was doing. She relaxed back into her seat, barely managing to rescue herself from complete embarrassment, and took some comfort in the thought that he hadn't noticed that she'd been about to stand as his attention was focussed on Lila.

The drive to go to him had been strong and the attraction she felt was primal, carnal and, while the result might have been pure embarrassment, it pleased her that she could still experience these feelings. That she still had the desire. The want and the need.

She couldn't remember the last time she'd felt such an immediate attraction to a man. She hadn't been remotely interested in men or relationships for the past two years yet somehow, with just one look, she knew she would change her mind for this man.

Who was he?

She checked for a hospital ID lanyard hanging around his neck but there was nothing. If he wasn't a doctor, who was he? Should he even be in the hospital?

He stepped into the room and crossed the floor, and Rose held her breath.

She was vaguely aware that Lila's giggles had stopped and out of the corner of her eye she saw Lila turn her head as she noticed the man's movements.

'Daddy!'

This was Lila's father?

He reached his daughter's bed and bent over, kissing her on the forehead. 'Hello, princess.'

Princess. Rose's father used to call her that. But she forgot all about her father as this man straightened up and looked at her.

Her breath caught in her throat, stuck behind a lump that had lodged there.

Now that father and daughter were side by side Rose noticed that they had the same eyes. Dark and serious. His chocolate eyes were intense, probing and forceful and she felt as if he could see right into her soul.

Mitch straightened up and looked again at the woman who sat by his daughter's bed. He'd noticed her as soon as he'd stepped into the room. He'd heard his daughter giggling, a sound he didn't hear enough of, but he'd been distracted by the woman sitting beside Lila's bed. She was not the type to go unnoticed.

He thought he'd imagined her at first. She didn't look real. Her face was round and serene, perfectly symmetrical. Her green eyes were enormous and iridescent. Her mouth was wide and her nose small. She looked like a woman from a Renaissance painting. Maybe that Botticelli one, the one of the young Madonna with the baby Jesus and the two angels. The light from the window bounced off her golden hair, making it shine like spun silk and making him forget that he hated hospitals, making him forget that he wished he and Lila were a thousand miles away. She was absolutely beautiful, but he had no idea who she was or why she was by his daughter's bedside.

She was watching him now, staring, silent, frozen like a deer in a spotlight. There was something fawn-like about her. Innocent. Young. Maybe it was her huge, luminous eyes.

Who was she?

She wasn't a nurse. She had a hospital ID badge hanging around her neck but she wasn't wearing a uniform and unless things had changed considerably since his last foray into a hospital he was pretty certain nurses didn't have time to sit idly at patients' bedsides. Unless the patient was critically ill, which he knew Lila wasn't.

A feeling akin to dread flooded through him as it occurred to him who she might be. 'Are you from social work?' he asked. The social worker had left several messages for him on the station answering machine but by the time he got in at the end of the day it was well past office hours and too late to call back. He knew he could have returned to the house during the day to make a call but he'd been nervous. Worried about what the social worker might want. Worried she might want to talk about what had happened two years ago. That she might want to talk about Cara. He had refused counselling before and had no qualms about doing it again. They didn't need it. They were all fine.

'I meant to call you back,' he fibbed.

She was frowning. A little crease had appeared between her green eyes, marring the perfect smoothness of her brow.

'I'm not a social worker,' she replied.

Mitch relaxed; expelling the breath of air he hadn't even been aware of holding.

'I'm Rose,' she continued. 'I'm just here to keep Lila company.' She stood up. Her hair fell past her shoulders and she lifted her hands and gathered it all, twisting it into a long rope and bringing it forward to fall over one shoulder.

Now it was his turn to stare. Her movements were fluid and effortless. She'd obviously done this a thousand times before but to Mitch it was one of the sexiest things he'd ever seen and he was transfixed.

'But now that you're here, I'll get going,' she said, and before he could find another word to say she had stepped past Lila's bed and was on her way out of the ward.

He couldn't stop himself from watching her go and his eyes followed her out of the room.

She was slim but under her dark trousers he could see the two, full, round globes of her buttocks. They bewitched him as she stepped out of the room. She wore a soft white top that floated around her torso and reinforced his first impression of her as a golden angel.

Or maybe a golden rose.

Rose who? he wondered. She had left without a decent explanation of who she was and why she was there.

She was young and pretty and her name was Rose. That didn't seem like enough information. He wanted more. But just thinking about her made him feel old. He couldn't remember ever feeling young. He felt like he'd always been old. He knew he'd only felt that way since he'd lost his wife but he struggled to remember how he'd felt before. So now it felt as if he'd been born old.

His life was defined by before Cara died and after Cara died. But the more time that passed the harder it was to remember the before. He was so busy running the station and trying to figure out how to be a single father that he never seemed to have time to stop and sit and remember her. He was asleep before his head hit the pillow at night and up at dawn and he didn't stop all day.

If he had time to stop he might realise he was lonely but this was not something he noticed on a day-to-day basis. He had got used to life on the station and the absence of his regular weekly trips into Broken Hill and he only noticed his loneliness when he visited the city. At the cattle station, despite its isolation, he was surrounded by people who knew him; some of the staff had worked for him for close to ten years. But in the city no one knew him and he knew no one. He could go all day without talking to a soul. Despite the fact that there were hundreds of people around him in the city he was alone with too much time on his hands.

He didn't enjoy the city but he was going to have to keep returning until he could take Lila home. Maybe he should make an effort to make some connections with people. Talk to people, to complete strangers. In the country he wouldn't hesitate but city people were different. He'd been one of them once but now he just felt disconnected. They seemed busier, more caught up in their own lives, existing close together but without any meaningful interaction. He was so used to sharing his day, his life, with his workforce. At least until dinner was finished but after that he put his children to bed and was now in the habit of spending his nights doing the bookwork before going to bed alone. It was becoming a sad existence. A self-perpetuating cycle.

His mind drifted back to Rose. Thinking about her was a pleasant distraction from the dozens of other things that had been occupying his mind of late. It had been a long time since a pretty woman had caught his eye. It wasn't as if he met a lot of new women in Outback Australia and he'd just about given up noticing. He was tired and jaded, so it was a pleasant change to notice a pretty woman and he almost felt human again. But he knew he didn't have time for anything more than an appreciative glance. His days were busy, too busy for romance.

And despite the pleasure that seeing a beautiful woman had given him, he couldn't imagine ever falling in love again. It wasn't worth the risk. He would have to recover as best he could and move on. Alone.

Next time he came to the city he would bring the boys with him, he decided. They wanted to see Lila, they were missing her, and now that she was on the road to recovery he knew she would like to see her little brothers too. He'd bring the boys and they would provide him with company. Then he wouldn't need to think about young, blonde, Botticelli angels called Rose. He wouldn't have time to wonder if he'd see her again.

CHAPTER THREE

'IS SHE ASLEEP?' Rose asked as her sister walked into the kitchen.

Scarlett had been settling her daughter, Holly, for her afternoon nap while Rose had chopped what felt like a mountain of cabbage and carrot to make coleslaw. But she'd been glad to have a job to do. She was hoping it would keep her mind busy so she would have no time to think about gorgeous men with kind faces and daughters in hospital. Lila's father had unsettled her. Her reaction to him had her on edge but she found if she kept herself occupied she could almost manage to push him to the back of her mind. Wielding a sharp knife was making sure she stayed focussed on the task at hand. She scraped the vegetables into a bowl and started tossing them together to make the salad.

'Yes,' Scarlett replied, 'but she was fighting sleep every step of the way. I think she has too much of her father in her—she knows there's a party going on and she doesn't want to miss out!'

Rose smiled. Her brother-in-law did like a party. He'd grown up in a big family; he was the youngest of six siblings so there had always been plenty of people in the house and even now he liked to surround himself with family and friends. There was no special reason for today's gathering but Jake never needed a reason. He loved a crowd and didn't mind being the centre of attention. He'd worked as a stripper to put himself through medical school and Rose had heard he'd been very good at it. She had no doubt he'd loved every minute of it. Scarlett, by comparison, was happy behind the scenes. She only needed the attention of one person, her husband.

Like Jake, the old Rose had loved a party too. She'd enjoyed attention and she knew she got more than her fair share, but now that attention made her uncomfortable. Now it only made her more aware of everything that had happened to her. Aware of the contrast between the pretty Rose of her youth and the new Rose. She felt much, much older than her twenty-three years. She'd been through a lot in the past two years and had come out the other side a lot less positive about the future. She knew now that some things were out of her control and just because *she* had a plan it didn't mean that *life* had the same one for her.

Things were different now.

Rose had been avoiding parties but Scarlett had refused to listen to any of her excuses. The only reason Rose had agreed to come to this barbecue was because Scarlett had threatened to withhold time spent with Holly if she didn't attend. It was emotional blackmail—Scarlett knew Rose couldn't bear to think of being separated from her niece. Holly was one of the few highlights in her life. One of the things that Rose had fought so hard for. She adored Holly and Holly adored her.

Having a family of her own was all Rose wanted. It had been all she'd wanted since she was eight years old. Her dreams had been so different from those of her two elder sisters yet now they were both married and Scarlett had a daughter. Scarlett and Ruby were living Rose's dream and Rose couldn't help feeling a pang of jealousy when she thought about it. Scarlett had professed that she was never going to have kids, she'd always intended to focus on her career, yet look at her now, Rose thought: a qualified anaesthetist and mother to the most adorable little girl.

Ruby, the middle of the three Anderson sisters, was a different kettle of fish altogether. She was nomadic, nothing remotely like Rose, who was the epitome of a homebody. Marrying Noah was the first ordinary thing Ruby had ever done, but even then she'd gone for the unusual. Not too many people were married to professional race car drivers. Ruby had always had a point of difference, whether it was her dress sense, her living arrangements or her boyfriends; no one could ever accuse her of being ordinary, whereas Rose longed for an ordinary life—a husband who adored her, perfect children and her own happily ever after.

She wanted to re-create that perfect world she used to live in. The world she'd inhabited until the age of eight. She wanted to fall in love and have her own family. She believed in true love and part of her still hoped it would happen for her. She still imagined her white knight would come and sweep her off her feet. He would give her the world and would be so blinded by love that he wouldn't notice all her flaws.

The Anderson sisters had grown up with their own labels. Scarlett was the clever one, the career girl; Ruby was the fun one, the slightly wild and offbeat sister; Rose, not overly ambitious, had been content to be the pretty one. Until recently.

She used to be so confident, used to be able to walk into a room and know that men would look at her. She knew she was pretty and her blonde hair and big green eyes lent her an air of innocence that men couldn't resist. But Rose didn't feel pretty any more. She was scarred, emotionally and physically, but she hated the idea of anyone else knowing it.

She was also scared. Scared that no one would want her now.

Scarlett kept telling her to give herself time. To get back out into the world without expectations. To relax, have fun and see what happened. Her psychologist was telling her the same thing—give yourself time—but Rose wasn't convinced that time was the great healer that everyone professed it to be.

It had been almost two years since her last relationship had ended and she didn't feel any closer to being ready for another one. Not when she knew she would have to open herself up.

She was scared and scarred and she didn't believe that was a combination conducive to finding love.

Scarlett held out a tray of burgers and shash-liks to Rose.

'Would you take these out to Jake for me, please?'

Rose could see her brother-in-law at the bar-becue, talking to one of his friends.

'I know what you're doing,' she said.

'What?' Scarlett replied, all wide-eyed and innocent.

'You want me to talk to Rico.'

'He's a nice guy.'

'I'm not saying he's not, but—'

'You're not ready.' Scarlett finished the sentence for Rose with her usual retort but that hadn't been what she was about to say. 'I'm worried about you, Rose. You need to get out there. You'd have fun with Rico. It doesn't necessarily have to be anything more than platonic fun but at least you'd be out and about. Working and spending time with Holly isn't enough. You're twenty-three, have some fun.'

Rose couldn't mount a good argument so she reached out and took the tray of barbecue meat, resigned to the fact that she would have to let Scarlett win this round. Scarlett won most rounds. She was the bossy older sister. Rose knew she did it out of love and so she gave in. It was easier that way. 'All right,' she sighed, 'I'll go and talk to him.'

She was aware of Scarlett watching her through the kitchen window as she stepped outside. She knew her big sister was worried about her. Scarlett had always mothered her. They had all suffered when Rose's father had died suddenly and their mother just hadn't coped with the aftermath. Scarlett, at the relatively young age of sixteen, had taken it upon herself to be the champion for her two younger sisters and that instinct had never quite left her, even though her sisters were now both adults.

Rose looked around, taking in Scarlett's house, small but filled with love, her gorgeous husband, and a garden overflowing with their friends. Despite the fact that Scarlett was eight years older than Rose, Rose couldn't deny that she wanted what Scarlett had. A career, a husband who adored her, and a baby. Actually, she would settle for two out of three; unlike Scarlett, she wasn't that interested in a career. She enjoyed teaching but it was a job rather than her calling, and she didn't have the same burning ambition about it that Scarlett had about her career as an anaesthetist.

And Rose knew exactly why Scarlett was pushing her to get outside and mingle. She had never made a secret of the fact that she dreamt of marriage and babies, certainly not to her sisters, but she wasn't sure that she was in the right frame of mind to mix and mingle today. Although she couldn't complain about the talent on offer. Jake's friends were lovely, a good mix of polite, gentle, charming and good-looking; many of them, including Rico, were professional men who were also former colleagues of Jake's from the strip club, The Coop. They took pride in their appearance without, for the most part, any vanity, and Rose was happy to appreciate the efforts they went to in order to stay fit and in good shape. But she wasn't sure that getting involved with one of her brother-in-law's mates was a good idea. What if things didn't work out? Wouldn't that be awkward?

Scarlett had insisted that Rico was a genuinely nice guy who treated women with respect. Rose knew she could do worse than go out on a date with him.

Not that he'd asked her yet, she chided herself as she crossed the paving and headed for the barbecue. She was thinking of excuses unnecessarily. Why would he be interested in her? Just because Scarlett had put the idea in her head it didn't mean that Rico was entertaining the same notion.

'Could I have your number?'

Rose had been chatting to Jake and Rico for several minutes when Rico asked the question. She was glad he'd waited until Jake had taken a tray of cooked hamburgers inside to Scarlett. She didn't think she had the heart to turn him down in front of his mate but she couldn't give him what he wanted. He was handsome in a swarthy, dark, Mediterranean way, he had a great body, hours in the gym having toned it to perfection, and he seemed genuinely nice, but there was no spark. Rose wondered if she'd ever feel that spark again. Rico was just the type of man she normally fancied, tall, dark, good looking, a few years older than her but she wasn't interested. She hadn't been interested in a long time.

Not quite true, she thought as she remembered a man with chocolate brown eyes, a triangular jaw and an easy smile. She might make an exception for a man like him. But that was just a silly fantasy about a complete stranger. She didn't even know his name.

'I'm sorry,' she said, 'I'm not dating at the moment.'

She knew she had to figure out how she was going to fulfil her dream of having a family when she didn't feel ready for a relationship. She still dreamt of finding love but in reality she was scared. She knew she couldn't wait for ever, she didn't *want* to wait for ever, but she was afraid to take that first step back into the dating game. She knew that first step would lead to others, which would lead to her having to share parts of herself, and that was the part she wasn't ready for.

Rico looked as if he might be getting ready to plead his case and Rose tried to remember how she used to turn invitations down without appearing rude. 'Why don't you give me your number?' she added. 'And if I change my mind, I'll call you.'

'Sure.'

'Great,' she replied, pleased he wasn't going to argue with her. 'I'll just grab my phone.'

She ducked inside and rummaged through her handbag. Her phone was lying in the bottom of the bag under a tin of coloured pencils she'd bought for Lila. She pulled the pencils out with the phone. She'd get Rico's number and then she would go and see Lila. She'd had enough of the party. She knew it would only be more of the same. Talking to Jake's friends, getting asked for her number. She made her excuses to Scarlett, promising to call back later, hoping that Jake's friends would have left by then and she could play with Holly without interruption.

But right now there was somewhere else she'd rather be. Someone else she'd rather talk to.

He was there.

He was sitting beside Lila's bed, his long legs stretched out in front of him, feet crossed at the ankles, watching as his daughter scrolled through what appeared to be photos on his phone.

She couldn't deny she'd been hoping to see him but now she was ridiculously nervous.

What had she expected? That she could just feast her eyes on him from a distance, hiding in the shadows without being seen herself?

That was exactly what she'd hoped. She hadn't thought about the reality of seeing him. Of talking to him. She wasn't ready to make scintillating conversation. She had nothing to say. She was completely out of practice.

But she couldn't stand in the doorway for ever. She crossed the room and the movement caught his eye. He lifted his head and his chocolate eyes followed her progress. He stood up as she got closer and Rose put another tick in the box that would be beside his name if only she knew what it was. He had manners. She adored men with manners. Having someone who would open a door for her or pull out her chair at dinner and seat her first, not because he thought she was incapable, just because it was a nice thing to do, always made her go weak at the knees. She always thought it gave a little glimpse about what he would be like as a husband or a lover. A mark of consideration and kindness. A man with manners would treat a girl properly.

'I didn't mean to interrupt,' she said. 'I just brought some drawing things for Lila.'

He smiled at her and Rose's knees wobbled as the ground tilted a little under her feet. She'd liked his smile yesterday when he'd looked at his daughter but that was nothing compared to having him smile at her. His face brightened and his brown eyes warmed and darkened like melted chocolate as he looked straight at her. 'You're not interrupting, Rose.'

A rush of happiness flooded through her and she could feel a faint blush stealing over her pale cheeks. He'd remembered her name!

She stopped next to Lila's bed before realising she should have continued to the opposite side. She was standing far too close to him. Her head barely reached his shoulders. If she turned her head towards him, all she could see was the powerful breadth of his chest; if she looked down she got an eyeful of a narrow waist and long, lean legs; if she breathed in she could smell him. He smelt clean and fresh as if he'd not long been out of the shower, and his scent overrode the antiseptic smell of the hospital.

Her heart was racing, making her hands shake. She wasn't sure why but he really unsettled her and she was unbelievably nervous. As she reached forward to pass the pencils and sketch pad to Lila the tin slid from her hands. The lid popped off as the tin hit the floor and pencils spilled around their feet.

His reaction time was faster than hers. He crouched down and gathered the pencils up as she stood there, trying to work out what had just happened. His head was level with her knees and she could look down onto the top of his head. His hair was cut short but it was thick and she had a sudden urge to reach out and thread her fingers through it. Instead, she curled them into a fist at her side.

He stood and handed her the pencils but the touch of his fingers sent a jolt of awareness through her that was so strong she almost dropped them a second time.

Maybe it had been a mistake, coming here. She was well and truly disconcerted and had lost all trace of coherent thought.

'I can't stay,' she said as she finally managed to put the pencils and sketch book on the end of Lila's bed. 'These are for you,' she said before she bolted for the door as fast as her disfigured feet would allow.

He followed her from the ward. She didn't turn around but she could feel him behind her. Her whole body was tense, her nerves taut, fighting against her as she tried to walk away.

'Wait!'

Her steps slowed of their own accord as he called to her and then he was beside her, his hand on her elbow, sending her heart crazy. She turned to face him.

'Thank you for getting those pencils for Lila. Can I reimburse you?'

She was looking into a pair of eyes that were so dark she could see her own reflection. Her eyes were wide, startled, and she knew that he had caused that look as his touch had sent her body wild.

He was waiting for her answer. She shook her head. 'No, I wanted to do it. I thought it would help to keep her occupied.'

'I meant to bring her things with me, she asked me to, but with all the other hundred things I had to organise to get away I forgot. Her brothers have been acting up, they're missing Lila and are upset with me for leaving them behind, and with all their carry-on I got completely distracted and forgot to pack Lila's things.' He paused to take a breath and gave her a half-smile along with a slight shrug of his shoulders. 'But you don't want to hear about all of that.'

Oh, but she did. She wanted to know everything.

'If you won't let me reimburse you, can I at least buy you a coffee?'

She gathered her hair in her hand and twisted it, bringing it forward to hang over her shoulder. She toyed with the ends, something she always did when she felt out of her depth. Keeping her hands busy helped to calm her down and it worked again now, giving her just enough breathing space to be able to reply. 'I don't even know your name.' As if it mattered. She already knew what her answer would be.

'It's Mitch. Mitch Reynolds.'

Mitch. It was perfect. The Reynolds part she had assumed but the rest of his name suited him perfectly. It was strong, straightforward and honest. He had an honest face and an honest name. He seemed like the type of man who could be trusted. He would call a spade a spade.

He put out his hand but Rose hesitated. She'd been thinking about him all night but even so her reaction to him today had surprised her. She was almost afraid to touch him again, afraid of what she would feel, afraid her body would betray her and he would be able to read on her face all the conflicting emotions that were coursing through her. Part of her wanted to see if she experienced the same sensation again but she knew she had to prepare herself first. If she was flustered she didn't want him to see. She needed to appear in control.

Almost against her better judgement she put her hand in his. His fingers closed around hers, his grip strong but not threatening, and Rose had the strangest sensation of familiarity, that her body already knew his touch. It certainly responded to it as though she'd had some knowledge, some experience, of him before.

'So now that we're no longer strangers, will you let me buy you a coffee? I wanted to talk to you about Lila.'

He had sounded so guilty about forgetting Lila's things; he'd sounded like he had the weight of the world on his shoulders and Rose couldn't deny she was desperate to know more. This could be her chance to find out.

She nodded, not trusting herself to speak. She didn't want him to guess how he affected her and she suspected her voice would be high and quavering. That was not the way to appear in control.

'The social worker stopped by the ward after you left yesterday,' Mitch said as he placed the cafeteria tray on the table and handed her a coffee. 'Did you have anything to do with that?'

Rose knew that the social worker had been trying to contact Lila's parents but she'd had nothing to do with the visit. She shook her head. 'No. I imagine she'd left instructions with the nurses to call her when you got here.' She took a bite of the doughnut that Mitch had insisted on buying for her and asked, 'Who came to see you?'

'Annabel.'

'What did she want?'

'She wanted to find out about Lila. Something about hospital policy for children who have no family support. Lila has family support, but I can't be in two places at once.'

Mitch didn't wear a wedding ring. She already knew that. She'd checked. She'd also done a little investigating yesterday after she'd left Lila's bedside and discovered that there didn't appear to be a Mrs Reynolds. Was that why Mitch needed to be in two places at once?

But surely Lila had a mother? She must have one. Rose wondered where she was. Wild horses wouldn't have kept her away from her own child if they'd been hospitalised and she thought it odd that she hadn't come to town, even if she wasn't part of Mitch's life any more.

If she wanted to know the answers, she would have to ask the questions. 'What about Lila's mother? Where is she?'

'My wife died, there's only me.'

'Oh.' That wasn't the answer she'd been expecting. Surely that was the sort of information that should have been passed on to her? But before she could say anything further, Mitch kept talking.

'So, if you're not part of the social work team, what is it that you do here?'

Obviously his wife, his dead wife, was not a topic that was up for discussion.

'I'm a teacher,' Rose replied, going with the subject change.

'A teacher?' Mitch queried. 'The social worker mentioned educational support... Are you what she was talking about?'

Rose smiled. His phrasing wasn't quite the way she would have put it. 'Yes, but not just me. We have a school here.'

'In the hospital?'

She nodded. 'Children who will have long hospital stays or frequent admissions, thereby missing school, can attend classes in the hospital. It stops them from getting too far behind and also keeps them socialising. We have a lot of kids, like Lila, from the country, and being away from family can be quite isolating. I imagine Annabel thinks Lila would benefit from attending classes.' Rose knew that was the case but she got the impression that Mitch wouldn't want to know the staff had been discussing him. She suspected he would want to feel like the idea and the decision to enrol Lila in the hospital school was his. 'I teach middle primary mainly.'

'So you would teach Lila?'

Rose nodded.

'How does it work? School of the air I'm familiar with, but that's about it for schools out our way.'

'We have several teachers on staff covering everything from kindergarten through to high school and we have several classrooms. If children can make it to the classrooms they attend there but we can also teach them in their beds.'

'And Lila can join in?'

'Yes. Any child who is going to be in hospital for longer than a couple of days or is admitted frequently can be enrolled and we work closely with their regular school to make sure what they are learning is relevant.'

'Why is this the first I'm hearing about this?'

Rose smiled. 'I would guess Annabel has been trying to tell you, and if you'd called her back you would know.'

'Touché,' he said, before taking another sip of his coffee. 'Lila would probably enjoy being in a classroom and having other kids her age around instead of just her younger brothers. How do I organise this?'

'You'll have to email Annabel and she can put a request in on your behalf,' Rose explained.

Mitch pulled out his phone, asked for Annabel's email address, and sent an email off straight away. He copied Rose in to the email and her phone beeped as the email hit her inbox. She glanced at her screen. Mitch's signature on the bottom of the email included the contact details for the station.

Emu Downs.

It sounded so romantic. 'Emu Downs. That's a beautiful name.'

Mitch smiled and Rose's heart soared. It was crazy how she reacted to his simple gestures. She'd spent months telling herself she wasn't ready for a relationship yet this man, virtually a complete stranger, was able to make her body spring to life.

'You're imagining huge mobs of emus running across the land, aren't you?' Mitch's question interrupted her fantasy.

Emus? She hadn't been imagining anything of the sort! But she couldn't tell him the truth— that she was feeling such a strong pull of attraction that she was amazed he hadn't noticed. She couldn't tell him the truth so she fibbed. 'I was. Are there lots?'

'Not any more. The dingoes and the drought have wiped a lot of them out.'

'It's a cattle station, is that right?'

Mitch nodded.

'Has it always been in your family?'

'It belongs to my wife's family.'

The dead wife. That brought her back down to earth with a thump. This man with the gorgeous eyes and kind smile had children and a dead wife. He ran a cattle station out back of nowhere and he'd told her he had a lot on his plate. Hooking up with a random girl was probably not high on his agenda.

But Rose couldn't shake the feeling that

fate had brought him to her. That they were supposed to meet, that there was *something* between them and that he was going to be important to her in some way.

Or maybe she was going to be important to him. He looked a little distracted, lost in his memories, and Rose instinctively wanted to help. She had a tendency to feel other people's pain. Perhaps because she'd suffered a major loss, the death of her father, at a young age, it had fine-tuned her empathy but she definitely felt as though she was the one who could help him. But how?

She wanted to reach her hand across the table and take his. Offer him comfort. But even she was able to realise how strange that would seem.

Before she had a chance to embarrass herself Mitch pushed back his chair and stood up. 'I'd better get back to Lila. Thanks for your company.'

He looked at her with his dark brown eyes and Rose knew he was seeing her now, he wasn't caught up in the past any more, and she thought he was going to say more but he simply came around to her side of the table and held her chair for her, waiting to pull it out as she stood. It seemed their coffee date was over.

'I'll speak to Annabel on Monday,' Rose said, 'and get Lila into classes.' If she was teaching

Lila she would possibly have an excuse, a reason, to keep in touch with Mitch. And for now that would have to do. And for now that gave her hope.

CHAPTER FOUR

ROSE HAD BEEN at the hospital bright and early on Monday. She'd quietly hoped that it might give her a chance to see Mitch but soon found he'd returned to the station the night before. She did, however, manage to get everything sorted for Lila to attend school and she would be joining in for the afternoon session today.

Rose had five other children in the class, all of whom had been in hospital for some time, and she introduced them to Lila.

'Okay, everyone, we have a new student joining us today. This is Lila, she lives in the Outback on a cattle station and normally does School of the Air so once Lila has settled in perhaps we'll find out more about her school and how different it is from the schools you go to. Lila, this is Skye, Elise, Tuan, Alistair and Jade.'

Skye and Elise suffered from cystic fibrosis and were regular inpatients who had become good friends. Tuan was in hospital being treated for leukaemia, Alistair was a post-op surgical patient and Jade had a gastro-intestinal disorder that required regular admissions but today they were simply Rose's students. Attending school gave them a chance to forget about their illnesses. What was wrong with them ceased to matter as they focussed on the tasks that Rose set for them and Rose loved helping them to feel like normal kids.

'This afternoon we are going to make posters,' Rose told the children. She had planned a simple project for them to start working on today. She hadn't yet spoken to Lila's School of the Air teacher to see what she was doing in class but this project would get all the children interacting and let Lila settle in. Lila had nodded to the other children when Rose had introduced her but hadn't said a word. Rose knew Lila didn't say much on the ward but she was hoping she might be inclined to chat to her peers. Maybe she just needed time. 'I want you each to choose your favourite zoo animal and we are going to research it. There are some facts I need you to include and then you can decorate your poster however you choose.'

She knew Lila would enjoy illustrating her poster and hoped that would help her to feel comfortable. Once she had a chance to settle in, perhaps then she'd start talking. 'I want to know why the animal is in the zoo. Is it for educational reasons or is the animal under threat of extinction or for some other reason? Where does the animal come from? Are there any left in the wild? What is its habitat, diet and predators and you can include any other interesting or unusual facts or characteristics.'

Rose wrote the required information on the whiteboard and handed out laptops and brightly coloured poster paper and there was much animated discussion as the children tried to decide on their favourite animal.

'Rose?' Alistair stuck his hand in the air. 'Lila wants to do her project on horses but they're not a zoo animal.'

'Actually, there are types of horses that are found in zoos,' Rose replied. 'Why do you want to do horses, Lila?'

'They're my favourite animal.'

'What about a zebra?' Jade suggested.

'No.' Lila's tone was definite and Rose thought she looked close to tears. She needed to find out what was wrong. She didn't want Lila's first day going pear-shaped.

'Okay, once you've chosen your animal you can start looking up the information.' The children all knew how to use the internet, better than Rose did, and she knew that would keep them busy for several minutes while she had a chat with Lila.

She pulled a chair out and sat beside Lila. 'Horses aren't really a zoo animal. You'll find it hard to give me the information I'm after if you choose horses.'

'But I'm worried about Fudge. I want to do a project on her in case I have to give her away.' Once again, Fudge seemed to be Lila's preferred topic of conversation.

'Why would you have to give her away?' Rose asked.

'Because of what happened.'

'But it was an accident. It wasn't Fudge's fault.'

'No, it was my fault.'

Rose remembered being eight years old and feeling like every bad thing that happened was a direct result of things she did. The sense that cause and effect were all controlled by your actions. When her dad had died she could remember thinking that if only she'd eaten all her peas or picked up her toys when he'd asked her to that he wouldn't have died. She doubted very much that the accident had been Lila's fault but she wasn't going to discount her fears. 'How was it your fault?'

'I should have checked that Ruff was tied up properly.'

'Who's Ruff?'

'He's our dog. He's not supposed to go near the stables. He barks and nips at the horses' heels and scares them. The boys tied him up but I should have checked. Sometimes the boys don't put his collar on tight enough and he slips his head out.'

Rose did her best to allay Lila's fears. 'I will speak to your dad and ask how Fudge is, make sure everything is okay. In the meantime, why don't you look up Mongolian horses?' She wrote down the name so Lila could spell it. 'They are special horses and some of them live in zoos. You might like to do your project on them. They aren't that different to Fudge.'

Rose called Mitch at lunchtime but only managed to reach an answering-machine. While it was good to hear his voice, even if it was only a recording, she really needed to speak with him. She left a message and her phone number and asked him to call her back. Lila was beginning to open up to her and she wanted to make sure she followed through with her promise to speak to Mitch. She didn't want to disappoint Lila, she didn't want to give her a reason not to trust her and to keep her thoughts to herself. Rose knew that Lila still wasn't talking much to the nursing staff, remaining a quiet, self-contained child, and Rose wanted her to feel that she would listen if she spoke.

* * *

It took three days for her call to be returned, by which time she had left three more messages. She'd planned on setting Mitch straight, explaining that his daughter needed to be one of his priorities and asking why it had taken him so long to call her back, but he cut off her argument before she'd had a chance to get started.

'Rose, I'm sorry it's taken me so long to get back to you. I've been away from the house. I had to repair some of the windmills and check stock.' He seemed to expect her wrath and that took the wind out of her sails.

'I left the first message three days ago!'

'I know but the windmills aren't outside the back door. The station is the size of Trinidad and Tobago, it takes a while to check them all and longer if I need to do repairs.'

Even his voice was enough to make her pulse skyrocket. She closed her eyes as she listened to him speak, letting the deep notes of his voice caress her soul.

His explanation made sense.

'Trinidad and Tobago?'

'That's about as big as Kangaroo Island.'

'Wow, I hadn't realised.'

'There's no reason why you should. But tell me why you rang. Is everything okay with Lila?'

'She's fine,' Rose reassured him, remembering the purpose of all the calls she'd made. 'She's doing well, enjoying the classes, but she is concerned about her horse.'

'Fudge? Why?'

'She's worried you might get rid of her horse because of the accident.'

'What? Of course not. Would you please re-assure her that Fudge is fine. Tell her Jimmy is taking good care of her and she'll be waiting for Lila when she comes home.'

'Sure.'

'Thank you. I should be around the home-stead now for the next few days at least, so will you call me if there's anything else? I promise to get back to you as soon as I can but it will usu-ally be late at night. It's the only chance I get to sit in the office and take care of the bookwork and any messages. I realise it's out of hours for you, will that be a problem?'

It wouldn't make any difference to her. He was calling on her mobile but chances were she'd be home anyway. She was tired at the end of the day. Being at work was taking more phys-ical effort than she had anticipated. She knew she would gradually get stronger and that her endurance would improve and she wasn't going to admit defeat, but at the end of the day she was more than happy to come home and put her feet up. Mitch could call at any time. She doubted he'd be interrupting anything important and she was more than happy to talk to him.

'You have my mobile number, you can call anytime.'

Mitch leant back in his office chair, stretched his arms over his head, and tilted his head from side to side, easing the tension in his shoulder muscles. He'd had a busy few days and today had been no exception. He'd spent the day repairing fences. It was tough, physical work even with all the modern machinery and he was looking forward to a long, hot shower, but first he wanted to call Rose before it got too much later.

He had taken Rose at her word and had been calling every few days on the pretext of checking on Lila but really that was just an excuse. He was worried about Lila but he realised he couldn't be in two places at once. He couldn't be away from the station indefinitely; even though his stocks were low he needed to oversee the cattle he did still have to make sure they were being properly looked after. He knew Lila was in good hands but her hospitalisation gave him a reason to pick up the phone and talk to Rose.

He wanted company. Female company. He spent his days in the company of men but in the days of old he'd been able to finish his day with a nightcap on the veranda with his wife, talking about their kids, the station, their future. Until that had all ended. He missed those days.

There was a shortage of women on the station and he noticed their absence. Ginny brought the tally to three, along with Shirley, the station cook, who was in her early sixties, and the station mechanic's wife. There was the occasional jillaroo on staff but they tended to come and go with the seasons.

He missed Cara but talking to Rose filled that gap. It gave him a sense of being connected to something bigger than him, bigger than the station. He missed the connection to another person.

He was lonely but there wasn't anyone who was going to replace Cara. He couldn't imagine ever falling in love again, it wasn't worth the risk. But all the same he didn't want to spend the rest of his life alone. He wanted company and for now Rose was giving him that company, even if it was only over a telephone line.

'How was your day?' Rose asked, after she had given him an update on Lila. This was what he missed, among other things, having someone to share the simple things, the everyday things with. Someone who knew his moods, could tell if he'd had a good day or a bad one just by the tone of his voice or the set of his shoulders. 'Did you get the fences fixed?'

He closed his eyes as he imagined her sitting down, talking to him. He pictured her in the outfit she'd been wearing on the day she'd brought the pencils to Lila. She'd looked gorgeous. She'd been wearing a loose top in a pale pink that had swung around her body and had left his imagination to fill in the gaps about what was hidden underneath, but she had paired the top with cut-off denim shorts that had shown off her amazing legs and hadn't required him to use any imagination at all. Her blonde hair had been loose and had cascaded in shiny waves over her bare shoulders. He could see her now, one hand holding the phone, the other playing with the ends of her blonde hair. Her hair had looked silken and soft and his fingers had itched to touch it and feel it for himself.

'I did,' he replied. He'd spoken to her two days ago, explaining that he might be out of reach for a day or two as he had to check some fences that had come down. Rose didn't need to know his whereabouts—the medical staff were the ones who might need to get in contact with him—it had just given him an excuse to call her. As it was, he had spent a day and a half mending fences before leaving a couple of his station hands to finish off the job tomorrow. He'd wanted to come back to the homestead, wanted to pick up the phone and talk to Rose, wanted to hear her voice. 'A camel train had been through.'

'Why is there a train line through one of your fences?'

Mitch laughed. He knew Rose enjoyed getting an insight into station life and he was used to the fascination that city folk had regarding Outback life, but he normally found it a difficult thing to describe. Somehow it was different with Rose. She asked questions that prompted him to recall different events and her easy laughter made him strive to recount the amusing aspects of his day. He wanted to amuse her. He loved hearing her laugh. Her laughter brightened his day and no matter what sort of day he'd had he always felt better once he'd spoken to her. 'Not an actual train full of camels.' He chuckled. 'I meant a herd of camels.'

'Oh.' Rose joined in with his laughter. 'I thought a group of camels was called a caravan.'

'I think there are a few different collective nouns and all of them would be far nicer than what I was calling them today; my fences were completely flattened.'

'Well, no one could ever say station life was dull.'

'No, it's far from that.' It could be lonely, he'd

admit, but it wasn't dull. 'But I could do without the camels, they're terribly destructive.'

'Can you build bigger fences?'

'I have hundreds of kilometres of fencing. I can't make it *all* camel-proof, it would cost a fortune and camels are pretty stubborn. They'd rather go through something than around it and I'd need pretty strong fences to stop them. If they're thirsty, once they smell water not much will keep them out. They're pretty big and can do a lot of damage *en masse.*'

'So when you have the camels under control, will you be coming to town again?' Rose asked.

He could hear the smile in her voice but what he wanted to know was, was she asking because she wanted to see him? Dared he hope she was enjoying the phone calls as much as he was?

'Lila is missing you,' Rose added, dashing his hopes.

He had already decided to get back to Adelaide as soon as possible. He needed to see Lila but he was also keen to see Rose. This was another reason for his call tonight. He'd wanted to let her know of his impending visit, wanted to make sure she'd be around.

'I'll be there on Friday. I'm bringing the boys this time.' It had been a couple of weeks since he'd last been down to the city and the boys had been pestering him to take them on the next trip.

'Lila will be thrilled. She's told me all about her brothers. She's missing them too.'

Mitch laughed. Rose's comments and observations often made him laugh. It was a good release, and he knew he hadn't laughed often enough over the past two years. It was good to talk to someone who hadn't known Cara, someone who didn't seem to think it was wrong to want to be happy. 'I'll remind her of that next time she complains that they are bugging her.'

'How long are you staying?'

'A few days. I need to see my accountant and take care of a few other business matters.'

'What will you do with the boys while you're in meetings?'

'I'm not sure. I guess they'll just have to come with me.'

'They can come to school if that's easier.'

'In the hospital?'

'Yes.'

'Are you sure?'

'Of course. Siblings of country kids are welcome at the school, it's no problem.'

'That would be fantastic. I'll see you on Friday, then.'

Mitch hung up the phone. He was excited. Excited at the prospect of seeing her again. It had been a long time since he had looked forward to anything with as much anticipation.

* * *

Heads turned as Rose and her sisters walked into the restaurant on Tynte Street. They were a striking trio. Scarlett, Ruby and Rose didn't really look alike yet they were all beautiful. Ruby and Rose had inherited their maternal grandmother's green eyes and all three girls had their mother's long legs.

This dinner had been in Rose's diary for weeks, scheduled to coincide with Ruby's visit to Adelaide, and Rose was secretly relieved that it had been booked for Wednesday night. She didn't want any commitments for the weekend. Mitch was coming to town and she wanted to keep her diary clear. Just in case.

They were shown to their table where the fourth member of their party was already seated. Candice stood up to greet her girlfriends, kissing each of them on the cheek. She was almost like their fourth sister. Like Ruby, she was a nurse and she had worked with both Scarlett and Ruby and had also grown up with Scarlett's husband, Jake.

'Drinks?' Scarlett asked the girls before the waitress left them to peruse the menu.

'Just water for me,' Ruby said. She didn't drink alcohol any more.

'Water is fine with me too,' Candice said.

Scarlett looked at Rose, who nodded. She

wasn't a big drinker, her body and her medications made it difficult to process alcohol. She was happy to start with water and maybe she'd have a glass of wine with her meal.

'What would people like?' Scarlett asked once their drinks were sorted. 'Shall we order a selection of the shared plates? That way we can try a bit of everything, including some vegetarian options for you, Ruby.'

'That sounds fine,' Candice said, 'as long as it's nothing with soft-boiled eggs or raw fish.'

'Oh, my God!' Ruby exclaimed. 'You're pregnant?'

Candice grinned. 'Yep, ten weeks, I know it's still early but I've been dying to tell you guys.'

Rose also had to avoid those foods. She wished it was because she was pregnant too, rather than for the real reason, which was to make sure she avoided infections. Although she had recovered from the bacterial meningitis she'd contracted, it had left its mark and she had to live with the after-effects. She couldn't afford to jeopardise her health by eating high-risk foods; it was safer just to cut out certain raw or undercooked foods from her diet.

'You and Jake need to have another baby now so mine can have a playmate,' Candice was telling Scarlett.

'We're trying.' Scarlett smiled. She looked so

content and serene, sometimes Rose was still amazed at the change marriage and a baby had wrought in Scarlett. She still loved her career but it was no longer the most important thing in her life.

'Ruby? What about you?'

'God, no. Our lifestyle doesn't allow for a baby.' Ruby's husband, Noah, was a professional race car driver. 'We travel the circuit for nine months of the year, can you imagine trying to do all that with a baby? I'd end up stuck at home or in a hotel room.'

'I can't imagine you stuck at home.'

'Neither can I.' Ruby laughed. 'So that means no babies for now. I'm not letting Noah have all the fun.'

'Congratulations, Candice, I'm really pleased for you.' Rose finally added her congratulations to her sisters'. She was happy for Candice but it didn't stop her from feeling a little melancholy. Everyone else was living the life she wanted.

'You'll be next, Rose.' Ever-observant Scarlett must have seen the wistful expression in Rose's eyes.

'Only because I'm the last one left.'

'Are you still leaving a trail of broken hearts in your wake?' Candice queried.

'No. I'm not dating.'

'Rico asked for her number,' Scarlett said.

'Oh, I remember him,' Ruby said. 'Has he called?'

'I didn't give it to him.'

'Why not?'

Rose shrugged. 'There was no spark.' She didn't want to waste time on someone who was unlikely to set her world on fire.

'You're not going to find your perfect man unless you get out there. Contrary to the fairy tales they're not going to arrive at your door on a white horse and carry you away to their castle.'

'I know that,' Rose protested. She didn't mind what colour the horse was. 'But do you really think love can grow if there's no initial spark of attraction?'

She wondered what colour horse Mitch rode. She couldn't help thinking of him. He'd called her often over the past two weeks and she was counting the days until he would be back in town. Only two more now. While Rico was nice, Mitch was another matter entirely. Just the sound of his voice and the tone of his laugh over the phone was enough to set her pulse racing. That was what she wanted. That was what she was waiting for. That feeling of excitement, of nervous anticipation. The sense that she couldn't wait to see him again and couldn't bare it if he didn't look at her, smile for her, touch her, kiss her. That was what she wanted in a man.

She looked each of the girls in the eye. She knew they understood what she wanted. She knew for a fact that they had all been knocked for a six the first time they'd laid eyes on their husbands.

'Noah was virtually unconscious the first time you saw him,' she said to Ruby, 'and you still knew there was something there.'

'That was my hormones.'

'Exactly. You felt it straight away. That's what I want. What if I'm out on a date with someone who I know could only ever be a friend and I miss my opportunity to meet "the one"?' She shook her head. 'I think I'll wait for the spark.'

'But what if the guy you're out with happens to be friends with the guy who will be "the one"? What if that's how you meet? You have to get back out there. You have to give yourself a chance of meeting him,' Candice said.

'Why don't you ring Rico? He knows a lot of people. Even if you don't think he's right for you, he has got lots of really nice friends,' Scarlett suggested.

'I don't think so.'

'Well, would you at least promise us that you'll consider going on a date with the next man who asks you out?'

Rose thought about Ruby's suggestion. If she wanted what her sisters and Candice had found, her own happily ever after, she would have to start living and stop hiding behind excuses. She'd been given a second chance at leading a normal life and she needed to start making the most of those opportunities. She needed to be open to the possibility of finding love. She was certain Rico wasn't the one but that didn't mean there wasn't someone out there who would love her even if she wasn't perfect any more, and when the time came, when that man appeared, she needed to be ready. It was time to start opening herself up. It was time to be brave.

'Okay, I'll consider it,' she said, and as she agreed to Ruby's request Mitch's face popped into her mind. Would he be the next person to ask her out? She crossed her fingers under the table. Could she be that lucky?

Despite arriving in Adelaide late the previous night, Mitch and the boys had been up for hours. It was force of habit to rise at dawn with the early morning chorus of birds and even in the city Mitch could hear the birds before the traffic noise started. He was at the hospital in time for the morning ward round as he wanted to chat to Lila's doctor in person and was relieved to hear her recovery was on track. He took the boys to breakfast while they waited for lessons to start.

Classes started at nine and Mitch was at the classroom door ten minutes later. He didn't want to appear too eager, too desperate but he also didn't want to wait any longer to see Rose.

She was leaning over one of the desks, talking to a student, her dark trousers stretched across her hips, and all Mitch could see was the round globes of her perfectly shaped bottom. His reaction was immediate but not altogether unexpected. He'd been thinking of her constantly for the past few days, eager to see her. She straightened up and turned when she heard the door close and Mitch stepped behind Jed, looking for some cover to hide his visceral response. It wasn't unpleasant but it was inappropriate for a classroom.

She smiled at him and crossed the room. She was glowing, she looked sunny and bright and suddenly Mitch's day seemed full of possibilities.

Rose squatted down to introduce herself to his sons. Her manner was natural, calm and relaxed and he could see the boys lapping up her attention. He knew exactly how they felt.

She took them each by a hand and walked with them over to Lila while Mitch stood by the classroom door, waiting like an expectant suitor standing in line for a chance to talk to her.

The boys were used to spending time amusing themselves; at home, they spent more time with their governess and the station cook than they did with Mitch and they didn't bat an eyelid at being left in Rose's care. They were used to having different people being responsible for them and they didn't seem to mind, but Mitch still felt a twinge of guilt that they were so independent at such a young age.

If Cara was still alive, would it be any different? The station staff were like one big family so Mitch suspected it might have been the same. Everyone would have looked out for the children regardless.

Rose used the couple of minutes that it took to get the boys sorted to get her racing heart under control. It was crazy that someone she barely knew could make her feel this way. Excited, nervous, tongue-tied. She'd been expecting him but that still didn't mean she was prepared.

She took a deep breath—inhale for four, exhale for eight—just like she'd been taught in hospital to calm herself down whenever things were getting on top of her. She took a second, deep breath as she walked back to Mitch, exhaling and trying to relax her muscles as she took in the sight of him waiting by the door.

He was wearing trousers and a long-sleeved buttoned shirt in a chambray blue that highlighted his tan. Once again he had riding boots on his feet. The leather looked well worn but it had been recently polished and Rose suspected that this might be as formal as his wardrobe got.

'Thank you for organising this. It will make the day so much easier,' he said with a smile, and Rose's heart immediately kicked up a gear, threatening to accelerate away, as her tongue tied itself in knots.

Something about him made her jittery, but in a good way. She couldn't put her finger on it, it was just a feeling. She felt alive, super alert, aware of every little thing and she didn't really want to get that feeling under control. She was enjoying it but she didn't want to appear skittish. She didn't want him to think she was young and ditzy.

Her tongue felt too large for her mouth as she tried to formulate a sensible reply. 'It was no trouble. I hope the boys enjoy it. I know going to school is probably not top of their favourite things to do in the city but hopefully the novelty of today, and the fact they get to spend time with Lila, will make up for it.'

'Trust me, it's far better for them than sitting

in my accountant's office. Better for me too. I thought I might take them to the beach for a swim and dinner tonight. If you're not busy, would you like to join us? Let me buy you dinner to say thank you.'

Even though she'd been hoping he might ask her out she'd managed to downplay her dreams, knowing it was unlikely to happen. She knew from their late-night phone conversations that he was a single dad with a lot on his plate—Lila, the boys, the station—but that hadn't stopped her from wishing for an invitation and she couldn't believe her wish had come true.

Despite only having had one real face-to-face conversation Rose felt as though she knew him well and it didn't seem odd that he'd invited her, a relative stranger. It seemed perfectly normal and because she'd been waiting, hoping for this invitation she wasn't about to turn it down.

'That sounds lovely. I'd like that.'

CHAPTER FIVE

MITCH AND THE boys met Rose in front of the hospital at the end of her day. The boys were dressed in swimming shorts and Mitch had changed out of his trousers and button-down shirt into a T-shirt and shorts. He had a back-pack slung over one shoulder but Rose wasn't paying much attention to that. She was distracted by a pair of very nice legs. Tanned and muscular, long and lean. He looked good in shorts.

Charlie was bouncing up and down on the spot, eager to get to the beach.

'Are you ready?' Mitch asked. 'I thought we'd take the tram, is that okay?'

'Of course.' The tram was something different and would take them directly from the city to the suburb of Glenelg, which had a beautiful beach and plenty of restaurants.

'The boys love the beach, that's one thing we don't have at home.'

Rose smiled. She could understand the attraction. The beach used to be a magical place for her too. She still found the salt air, the waves and the sunshine therapeutic, even if she tended to stay out of the water these days. She fell into step and they walked through the parklands towards the city.

The sun was low in the sky but there was still plenty of daylight left and the autumn air was warm. Mitch bought ice creams as they got off the tram and they ate them as they walked to the beach.

They found a spot not far from the jetty and Mitch pulled a towel from his backpack and spread it on the sand. The boys tore their shirts off, threw their shoes in a pile and ran straight into the water.

'Are you coming in?' Mitch asked as he stripped off his T-shirt. Rose's breath caught in her throat. Again.

He was seriously ripped. He looked lean when he was dressed, and he was, but undressed she could see that every muscle was exquisitely defined. She couldn't see one ounce of fat but she could see the perfect definition of his deltoids, biceps and abdominals. Riding around looking after his cattle must be good exercise. He was in unbelievable shape.

'I…' She couldn't think of what to say. She

couldn't think at all when he was standing semi-naked in front of her. He looked incredible. This was far better than anything her imagination had conjured up, and she'd been imagining plenty. She was in serious trouble. 'I—I don't have bathers,' she stammered as she tried to stop ogling a man who had no reason whatsoever to be interested in her.

'Just roll up your trousers, the water is beautiful. You can at least get your toes wet.'

No way! Rose baulked. That wasn't going to happen. That would mean taking her shoes off. She shook her head. 'I'm fine here,' she said as she flopped down onto the towel. 'I have to finish my ice cream.'

'Okay. You know where we are.'

She nodded and squinted into the westerly afternoon sun as she watched Mitch walk down to the sea. He took Charlie's hands and helped him to jump over the small waves as Jed duck-dived under them. The sound of laughter carried to Rose on the light breeze. It was a glorious afternoon and she was more than happy to soak up the sunshine and relax.

She finished her ice cream and stood up and walked to the water's edge. The sea was sparklingly clear and she longed to take her shoes off and feel the ocean but it wasn't going to happen, not with crystal-clear water, there was

absolutely nowhere to hide and she wasn't prepared to risk it. She walked to the jetty and back
instead, the setting sun hot on her shoulders.

She sat on the sand. Scooping it up, she let it
trickle through her fingers. She wanted to feel it
under her feet. She could keep an eye on Mitch
and the boys from where she sat. She'd have
time to get her shoes back on before they could
reach her. There was no one else nearby so she
slipped off her shoes and wriggled her feet into
the warm sand, making sure her toes were hidden. She sat and watched Mitch. He was standing deeper in the water now with his back to her.
The sun silhouetted him against the blue sky,
highlighting his broad shoulders, narrow waist
and long legs. The boys were taking it in turns
to stand on Mitch's hands and let him lift them
out of the water before he launched them into
the sea off his makeshift diving board. From a
distance Rose could imagine his muscles flex-
ing and relaxing as he picked up the boys. She
could remember her father doing the same with
her when she was little.

She heard Mitch calling to Jed. 'Last turn,
then I'm hopping out.'

She brushed the sand off her feet, using
Mitch's towel to quickly wipe the sand from between her toes and over her scars. Her feet were
warm and the sand stuck to her skin, she wasn't

going to get it all off in time. Her heart was racing. She'd have to put her shoes on, sandy feet and all. A few grains of sand in her shoes was preferable to exposing her feet to the scrutiny of others. She shoved her right foot into her shoe and tied the laces just as the boys ran up the beach towards her.

'Can we make a castle and a moat?'

Mitch had followed behind them and he replied, 'Sure,' as he pulled another towel from the backpack and started to dry himself off.

Rose wanted to look elsewhere but found it impossible. Even as she pulled her left shoe on her eyes were drawn to him. He was standing next to her and she looked up as he towelled his hair dry. The towel covered his face and she took the opportunity to check him out. His shoulders were broad, his arms muscular, his chest and abdominals perfectly sculpted. There was a dark 'V' angling down from his neck where his skin was more darkly tanned but that stark contrast just served to highlight his chest, which, while olive toned, obviously hadn't had the same sun exposure. The water droplets on his skin glistened in the sun before they were swiftly mopped up.

He dropped the towel on the sand and sat beside her. His knees were bent and he leant forward, resting his forearms on his kneecaps as he watched the boys constructing their moat. Jed had commandeered a bucket and spade from Mitch's bag and had sent Charlie running backwards and forwards to the sea as they tried to fill the moat but the water seeped into the dry sand faster than Charlie could bring it back.

Mitch turned his head to look at her. 'The boys said they had fun in the classroom today.'

She smiled. 'I think the beach might trump that, though.'

'Possibly,' he said as he shrugged his gorgeous shoulders. 'You can't win them all, I suppose. It must be an interesting job, though. Do you enjoy it?'

'I love it but it's pretty new still, I've only been working there for a few months.'

'Is it a long-term proposition?'

'I'm not sure.' It was actually only a relief position as she was covering another teacher's maternity leave, but there was no need to go into detail about that. She wasn't sure what she would do when the contract ended but she hoped she might get offered another one. She had no great aspirations to do anything else. She didn't want to travel the world like Ruby neither did she have massive career goals like Scarlett. She enjoyed being a teacher but one of the biggest attractions for her was that it was something that she could continue to do once she was married with a family of her own. That was her ultimate goal. Even with the dramas of the past two years, her dreams for the future hadn't changed. She hadn't suddenly developed a desire to see the world or climb mountains or save the planet—her illness had just intensified her desire for a family of her own, but she was reluctant to share that with Mitch.

Rose wasn't quite meeting his eyes any more and Mitch knew there was something she wasn't telling him. He shouldn't be able to tell, he barely knew her, but she was twisting her hair in her fingers again and already he knew that was a sign that she was uncomfortable.

She let her hair fall over her shoulder and the wind picked it up, blowing it across her face. She brushed it aside and looked out to sea. The wind had strengthened. Mitch saw grains of sand swirling along the beach.

'There's a storm coming,' Rose said.

Mitch looked out across the gulf. Clouds had gathered to the west and he could see ghostly fingers stretching from the clouds to the sea, the tell-tale streaks of rain. The water was getting rougher too, there were whitecaps further out in the gulf, dancing on top of the waves as they spread towards the beach, moving closer with the wind.

'We need to get off the beach in case it's an electrical storm,' Rose added.

'Let's go and get something to eat,' Mitch suggested. The boys had given up trying to fill the moat and instead were busy constructing extra towers for the castle. He didn't think they'd object to moving if food was being offered. He started gathering towels and buckets and spades. 'Fish and chips, burgers or pizza?' he asked as the boys looked up.

'Pizza!'

They collected their things but the storm was faster than they were and by the time they were crossing the grassy strip between the beach and the shops the rain was pelting down, hammering on the tin roofs of the buildings and pouring down the street.

Charlie froze as the wind and rain buffeted him from behind.

'Come on, Charlie, it's only water.'

His lip quivered. Mitch wrapped an arm around his waist and lifted him onto his hip, hurrying to get out of the weather. The backpack slipped off his shoulder and Rose reached out and grabbed it, taking it from him, lightening the load.

'Is he okay?' she mouthed at him over Charlie's head.

'He hasn't seen rain before.'

'Seriously?'

'It hasn't rained on the station for three years,' he said as he stepped under the protection of the shop verandas. 'The last time it rained he was just a baby.' There were other things Charlie was too young to remember as well and Mitch still wasn't sure if that was a blessing or a curse.

He stopped under the shelter but didn't put Charlie down. 'It's okay, buddy, we're safe here. A bit wet, though.'

They were all drenched. It wasn't such a big deal for him and the boys as they were still in their bathers but Rose was a different story. She had raindrops caught on her eyelashes and her hair was soaking wet but somehow she still managed to look beautiful. Her shirt clung to her skin, outlining every curve. Mitch wasn't sure where to look so he turned his gaze to the street, looking for somewhere to eat. Somewhere to escape to.

'Let's find somewhere to dry off,' he said as he continued to walk down Jetty Road. He took refuge in the first pizza bar he found. The boys needed feeding and he needed to take a breath.

'I'm just going to duck to the ladies' room. I need to dry off and there should be a hand dryer in there.'

That sounded like a good idea to Mitch. The

sooner Rose's clothes were dry the sooner he'd be able to concentrate again.

By the time she returned he'd got the boys settled at a table. Rose had dried off a little. Her shirt wasn't clinging to her any more, which was a bit of a shame in his opinion, but at least he could now focus on the menu. It was pretty simple, pizzas and some pasta dishes, but he knew he would have had trouble deciphering even that much with Rose sitting across from him looking like a contestant in a wet T-shirt competition.

'What would you like to eat?' he asked, handing her a menu.

'What are you having?'

'Meat lovers for the boys, we've got to keep the cattle farmers in business, and seafood for me. You're welcome to share either of those.'

'I think I'll have a Margherita,' she replied, without even glancing at the options.

'Are you vegetarian?' he asked. He was disappointed to think she might be; vegetarians were not a good fit for him. He tried to tell himself that he wondered about everyone and their carnivorous habits but he knew that wasn't true.

Rose shook her head. 'No, I just feel like a Margherita,' she said as the waitress put a jug of water and four glasses on their table. Once he'd placed their order she picked up the thread of their earlier conversation. 'How do you manage on the station for three years without rain?'

'There's a creek—a river, really—running through the property, but it's dry now. Luckily we also have artesian bores but I'm having to decrease stock and if we don't get rain soon we'll be in real trouble.'

'You said the station is about the size of Kangaroo Island. How big is that exactly?'

'One million acres.'

'Wow!'

'Have you ever been to the Outback?'

'No.' Rose shook her head. 'I haven't travelled much at all but I have been to Queensland's Sunshine Coast to visit my sister.'

'That's pretty,' he told her, 'but nothing remotely like our part of Queensland. We have wide open spaces and enormous blue skies. You can see for ever.' People always mentioned the wide open space but, for Mitch, it was the sky that he missed when he was away from home. 'You get the same colour sky down here but for some reason you can't see as far. I think it's the haze of the city. We get a lot of dust but when it settles the air is clear and clean. When people imagine the Outback they think of the colour red, and it is red, redder than you can picture, but there are plenty of other colours too. Blue and green, grey and white. The pink breasts of the galahs. The yellow of the sulphur-crested cockatoos. Purple and orange sunsets. Bright green tree frogs.'

'It sounds beautiful,' Rose sighed.

'It is.' As difficult as it could be at times, Mitch couldn't imagine leaving. There were a number of reasons keeping him there but one was the fact that he did love it. There really was no place like it.

Mitch looked sad. From her seat Rose could see out to the street, looking east towards the hills. The sun came out and she could see a rainbow form in the moisture that still blanketed the hills.

'Charlie, come with me, there's something I want you to see.' She stood up and held out her hand for Charlie; she was counting on the fact that Mitch would come too and she would be able to distract him from his sombre thoughts.

Charlie hopped up from his seat and took her hand. The sky over the ocean was clear again, the rain clouds having moved east, and there was a bright rainbow over the hills. Rose turned Charlie so he faced east. If he'd never seen rain, she was certain he would never have seen a rainbow and this one was fabulous. It was strong and crisp and she could clearly see six of the colours, and imagined she could also just make out a narrow band of indigo.

She pointed to the sky. Charlie's mouth dropped open and he turned to Mitch who, as Rose had hoped, had followed them outside.

'Dad, Dad, look, it's a rainbow.'

'Isn't it beautiful?' Rose said. Charlie's expression was priceless, a combination of surprise, delight and enchantment, and Rose turned around, unable to resist seeing Mitch's reaction to his son's glee.

'Yes, it is,' he replied.

Rose had expected him to be looking at Charlie or the rainbow but he was staring at her. She felt herself blush under his gaze.

It had been a long time since he'd seen anything so beautiful, Mitch thought as Rose looked at him. The sun shone on her face, making her glow, turning her golden and reminding him of the day he'd first met her.

She was twisting her hair around her fingers and he realised he was staring, making her uncomfortable. She broke eye contact, turning back to the hills and squatting down beside his son. 'Tell me what colours you can see, Charlie.'

All Mitch could see were two blonde heads together. Any stranger watching this scene would have mistaken Rose and Charlie for mother and son. He felt a pang of loneliness; Charlie barely remembered his mother.

Mitch missed Cara but more than that he

missed having company. He thought the children were doing okay; they couldn't miss what they didn't remember, right? But deep down he knew that something was lacking in their lives. Female attention. They all missed it, him included, even if they weren't knowingly aware of it. It was an innate, unconscious need that lived within all of them.

But he was thinking about more than what was missing from *their* lives. He was thinking about what was missing from *his* life. More specifically, he was thinking about sex. He'd been thinking about sex a lot lately, ever since he'd met Rose. It was something he enjoyed but he'd got used to it not being a regular part of his life. Since meeting Rose he couldn't seem to *stop* thinking about it.

He felt Jed's hand seek his. His son tugged on his fingers, seeking attention and providing some distraction from some untimely thoughts. 'Can we look for the pot of gold?' he asked.

'The end of the rainbow is a long way away, Jed,' Mitch replied as he noticed the waitress bringing pizzas to the table, 'and your dinner is ready. It's time to eat.' Time to concentrate on a different simple and basic need. Food was as basic and simple as sex but he couldn't afford to be thinking about sex. He had children to look after.

The boys tucked into their pizza with gusto. The fresh sea air, the water and the exercise had made them ravenous.

Rose took small, deliberate bites and talked while they ate. 'When do you think you might be able to take Lila home?'

'I'm not sure. We're a long way from any rehabilitation services so that is going to affect her discharge. It would be a completely different story if we lived in the city.'

'How far are you?'

'It's a five-hour drive, one way, to the nearest hospital and physio, which makes it difficult. We're used to those distances, everything is far away, but it will mean an overnight stay every time Lila needs an appointment so realistically she won't be discharged until she doesn't need intensive physio. Even our next-door neighbours are three hours away.'

'That makes it tricky to borrow a cup of sugar.' Rose smiled.

Mitch laughed. 'We've become experts at ordering supplies. The truck only comes once a month although that's one benefit of the drought, the trucks can get through.'

'It sounds very isolated—don't you get lonely?'

He did get lonely but he wasn't about to admit it. 'It's not as isolated as you might imagine.

There are about fifteen people living on the station with me, not counting my kids.'

'Fifteen! Why so many?'

'We have to be reasonably self-sufficient so there's the children's governess, the cook, a mechanic and his wife, and a pilot as well as the station hands. So there's plenty of company and there's always something happening somewhere nearby if we get cabin fever.'

'By nearby you mean several hours' drive away?'

He nodded. 'Mostly. But we're used to that.'

'How long have you lived there?' Rose asked as she picked up another slice of pizza.

'Almost ten years. We moved there after my wife's brother died. He was killed in a car accident and Cara's mum was diagnosed with breast cancer around the same time so they moved to Brisbane for treatment and there was no one else to run the station. We had to move. Cara's mum died just before Lila was born.'

'And your father-in-law? Where is he now?'

Mitch didn't mind talking about the circumstances that had led to him living on the station. The boys weren't paying any attention to their conversation, they were far too engrossed in their pizza and talking about people they had never met, or barely remembered, wasn't going to bother them. 'Also gone. He had a heart attack about eighteen months ago but I think he really died of a broken heart. After he lost Cara his entire family was gone, other than the grandchildren, and I think he just gave up. I'd asked him to come back to the station but he'd said he couldn't face it. Too many memories.'

'That's been a tough few years for you.'

Mitch preferred not to think about it. He preferred to keep busy, which didn't leave time to dwell on the past. But seeing it from an outsider's point of view it did sound stressful. No wonder everyone kept wanting him to have counselling. But talking about the basic, straightforward facts was one thing, talking about his feelings was another matter entirely. He was doing fine, the kids were fine, everything was okay. Loneliness wasn't a disease.

'What about *your* family, where are they?' Rose continued when he didn't reply to her earlier comment.

'Scattered,' he replied as he picked up the last piece of his pizza, surprising himself. He'd barely noticed that he'd been eating. 'We grew up in Mt Isa. Dad was an engineer on the mine, my siblings and I all went to boarding school and now we're spread everywhere. My parents retired to Townsville, I have one sister in Perth and another in Singapore. The station might technically be the halfway point but it's not easy to get to so we don't catch up all that often.'

The boys had demolished their pizza but were now both yawning. Charlie looked as if he was about to fall asleep at the table. Mitch was enjoying himself, and he couldn't remember when he'd last felt so relaxed. Rose was easy company, a breath of fresh air, but if he didn't get the boys home soon the evening was likely to go downhill very quickly.

He paid the bill and hailed a taxi to take them back to the city. By the time they were dropped at their short-stay apartment both boys had fallen asleep. Rose offered to carry Charlie inside and Mitch picked up Jed. He put them to bed and offered Rose a cup of tea. Anything to prolong the evening.

'Do you have any hot chocolate?' Rose asked.

He could see goose-bumps on her arms, and she was obviously feeling the cold. It was then that he noticed that her shoes were still wet from the earlier downpour.

'Sure,' he replied, looking at her feet. 'Why don't you take your shoes off? I'll stuff them with some newspaper to dry them out.'

'No, it's fine. It can wait till I get home.' Her feet were cold and uncomfortable and she couldn't wait to get her shoes off but there was no way she was going to do that in front of Mitch.

'Are you sure?'

'Positive.' She drank her hot chocolate as quickly as possible and made her excuses. 'I should get going,' she said as she stood up from the small kitchen table. She wasn't in any hurry to say goodnight but she needed to get out of her shoes. 'I'll call a taxi.'

'Can you drive a manual?' Mitch asked.

'Yes.'

'Why don't you take my car?'

'No.' Rose shook her head. 'I can't do that. You might need it.'

'The hospital is only around the corner. There's no other reason I would need it. If I could I would drive you but I can't leave the boys on their own. It will make me feel better if you take it.'

Mitch had stood up too. He was standing very close to her. If she reached out a hand she'd be able to touch him. She lifted her chin and looked up at him. He was watching her with his dark eyes and for one crazy moment she wondered if he was about to kiss her…

But he didn't reach for her, he reached to his left and picked up his car keys.

'Bring it back to me in the morning on your

way to work,' he said as he handed her the keys. 'That way I know I get to see you again.'

Rose floated home. Okay, so he hadn't kissed her but he wanted to see her again! That was almost as good.

'The kettle's just boiled, have you got time for a cup of tea?' Mitch asked when she arrived back at the apartment the following morning.

'That sounds lovely, thank you,' she said as she took the same chair she'd had last night. 'White and one.'

'The weather bureau is forecasting more rain for tomorrow,' Mitch said as he put her tea on the table. 'I'm thinking of taking the boys to an indoor trampolining venue. They love trampolines, but I won't let them have one at home. They're way too dangerous.'

'And horses and motorbikes aren't?' Rose asked. She knew Mitch allowed the children to ride horses and motorbikes and she couldn't see what the difference was. Horse-riding was obviously dangerous, it had put Lila in hospital.

'Growing up on a station they're going to be exposed to motorbikes, cars and horses so they need to understand the risks and learn how to manage them. Trampolines are a different story. More children end up in hospital from trampoline accidents than from horse-riding and motorbike accidents.'

'And you don't think that's because more children have trampolines, so statistically it's going to happen more often?'

'Fair point,' he conceded, 'but it doesn't mean I want to invite an accident. But I wanted to invite you to come with us.'

Rose thought it sounded like fun but she already had plans. 'I have to look after my niece tomorrow. Scarlett is working and her husband is on nights so he'll come home and sleep for the morning while I look after Holly.'

'We'll go after lunch, then,' he declared. 'We can spend the morning with Lila and I'll book a time for the afternoon. How does that sound?'

'Perfect,' she said.

Mitch checked them all in at the front counter and handed them each a pair of socks with rubber soles.

'What are these for?' Rose asked.

'Trampolining socks,' he said. 'A safety requirement. Apparently they stop you from slipping on the mats.'

Once again, Mitch had chosen an activity that involved her taking her shoes off. First the beach, then getting her shoes wet in the storm. How many more times could she avoid the situation? She held the socks in her hand as she tried to figure out a way around this latest dilemma.

She went to the toilets and changed her socks. It might seem like odd behaviour but she couldn't think of any other way around it if she didn't want to expose her feet. She checked to make sure her feet looked relatively normal in the rubber-soled socks; if her missing toes were obvious she would have to make excuses not to jump, but the socks were black, the same colour as the trampolines and, she hoped, with the constant movement no one would notice her misshapen foot. She put her shoes back on, only removing them again to store them in a locker when it was their turn on the trampolines.

The boys launched themselves from the viewing platform at one end of the massive trampolines onto adjacent mats. Rose hesitated, not quite sure of the approach etiquette for those past their teenage years. Mitch jumped down onto a third mat and held out his hand to her.

Rose took it, prepared this time for the shock of awareness that bolted through her.

The boys were happily doing flips on their trampolines, calling out constantly for Mitch to watch them. Rose bounced a little more sedately but despite her cautious technique she fell over several times. Her balance was appalling—trampolining was obviously not a sport for someone who was missing a few toes.

'I don't think I'll be trying out for the Olympics any time soon,' she joked after a few minutes of unsuccessful bouncing. 'I think I might have a rest.'

Mitch helped her off the mat and they moved back to the viewing platform from where they could watch the boys, who were now trying to bounce and throw basketballs through a hoop. Watching the boys was more fun than trying to master the art of trampolining for herself.

'I'm going to grab a bottle of water—can I get you one?' Rose asked.

She stopped at her locker and quickly changed her socks after buying the water. She didn't intend to jump again and she knew she would feel more comfortable once she had her shoes back on. She hooked her handbag over her shoulder and went to lean on the railing next to Mitch.

'Are you okay?' he asked when she returned.

Rose frowned. 'Why do you ask?'

'Your balance was a bit off.'

'I'm just clumsy.'

'You're not dizzy? You don't have a headache or earache?'

'No, I'm perfectly fine,' she replied, hoping he wouldn't catch her out in a little white lie.

'Are you sure? Because a few other things have caught my attention…'

Rose's heart beat a rapid tattoo in her chest. Oh, God, was this when he was going to tell her he'd noticed her foot? Was he going to ask her what had happened? She swallowed nervously and asked, 'Like what?'

'You drink a lot of water and go to the bathroom often and my sixth sense says it's more than clumsiness.'

Sixth sense? What was he talking about?

She let her gaze wander around the venue as she debated whether she should ask him to explain. Was that inviting questions that she wouldn't want to answer? Did she want to open that door?

She didn't think so but before she could make a firm decision her attention was diverted by another jumper making a very ungainly landing. She heard her own sharp intake of breath as she waited for him to get to his feet.

Mitch looked sideways at her as she gasped.

'What?' he asked.

She pointed to the trampoline at the far end of the cavernous building. 'That man! He just flipped backwards and landed on his head and now he's not moving.'

The man lay face down and motionless on the trampoline and everyone else around also appeared frozen to the spot. Rose was aware of a collective holding of breath as they waited to see what would happen next. Someone had to do something.

Another young man on the adjacent trampoline stepped across and knelt beside him. He looked as though he was going to try to turn him over.

'Stop!'

Rose almost jumped out of her skin as Mitch bellowed beside her and she was aware that Jed and Charlie had stopped jumping and turned to look up at the sound of their father's voice, obviously thinking they had done something wrong.

Mitch broke into a run. 'Don't move him!' he yelled as he sprinted along the viewing catwalk and headed for the stairs.

Rose saw the young man hesitate and look up to where Mitch was racing along above him. Everyone in the entire centre had stopped in their tracks, paralysed by the urgency in Mitch's voice.

Rose wasn't sure what she should do. Should she supervise the boys or follow Mitch? She glanced at the boys. They would be okay for a few minutes, they'd be better off continuing to shoot hoops. 'It's okay, boys,' she called down to them, 'keep playing.' Then she took off after

Mitch. Not at a run, she couldn't manage that, but she followed as fast as she was able.

By the time she reached floor level Mitch was already on the trampoline with the injured jumper.

'What's his name?' he was asking.

'Jason.'

He put his hand very gently on Jason's shoulder. 'Jason, can you hear me?' he asked.

There was no response.

Mitch moved his hand around to Jason's neck and rested his fingers over his carotid artery before carefully sliding his fingers under his nose.

'Call an ambulance,' Mitch said to no one in particular.

The staff seemed hesitant and unsure. Rose had her phone in her bag. She pulled it out and punched in the numbers, it would be faster for her to call 000 and then Mitch could talk to the dispatch centre. She didn't know how but he seemed to know what he was doing.

'Do you have a neck brace?' he asked a staff member as she waited for the call to connect. She was put through to the ambulance service and gave the address details and passed the phone to Mitch. 'They want to talk to you,' she said. 'Can you do that or do you want me to relay messages?'

Mitch reached for the phone. 'He's unconscious but breathing,' he said. 'Possible spinal injury. It's a priority two.'

There was a pause while the dispatcher was talking.

'I'm a doctor,' Mitch responded.

Rose blinked and listened for more. Had he just said he was a doctor?

'Yes, I'll stay on the line,' he said.

'What are you doing?' she couldn't help but ask as Mitch continued to kneel by the unconscious man. What was going on?

Mitch looked across at her. She was standing on the floor and from where he knelt on the trampoline their eyes were level. His eyes were dark and unfathomable and Rose wasn't sure that he was even seeing her properly. He certainly didn't answer her question.

'Can you get the boys and get them changed?' he said. 'Wait in the car for me, the keys are in the locker.'

Rose knew he wanted his children out of the way when the ambulance arrived. Her questions could wait.

She had to wait longer than she wanted; she didn't get to ask anything further until they were back at Mitch's apartment. He'd told her Jason had regained consciousness. He was still worried about a spinal injury but the ambulance had left the venue without sirens and flashing lights so hopefully it wouldn't be as bad as he'd first anticipated. He'd told her all that but he hadn't mentioned the thing she really wanted to know about.

'Are you going to tell me about the rest of it?' she asked. 'What happened back there? You're a *doctor*?'

'I *was* a doctor,' he replied.

Was, he'd said, not *am*. 'How do you stop being a doctor?'

'It's a long story.'

Rose saw a flash of something in his dark brown eyes. Was it pain, sorrow or regret? She wasn't sure but she wondered what the story was.

She opened her mouth to ask the question but he cut her off before she could speak. 'Let's just say it's not compatible with station life. But…' he shrugged '…it doesn't mean I've forgotten everything I learnt. That's why I was asking if you were all right before Jason's accident. I noticed your balance was a bit off and I was worried.'

The sixth sense he'd mentioned. Only it wasn't a sixth sense, it was seven years of medical school and who knew how many years of practising medicine. Rose couldn't believe what she was hearing.

'So, are you okay? Any headaches? Dizziness?' he asked again.

Rose shook her head. After the afternoon they'd had he was still going to quiz her on her health?

'I don't have a headache. I'm not dizzy or nauseous. There's nothing sinister going on. I'm fine now.'

'Now?'

Rose nodded. Knowing he was a doctor changed things a little—it would be less awkward explaining it to him. 'I only have one functioning kidney,' she told him, 'and it isn't mine.'

Mitch frowned and then she saw him do the maths. 'You had a kidney transplant?'

She nodded again.

'When?'

'Eighteen months ago. I contracted bacterial meningitis two years ago. I was in a coma for nine days but while I survived my kidneys didn't fare so well.'

Her transplant wasn't a secret. She was happy to talk about it. She'd discussed it often enough with her counsellor and with children in the hospital and she felt comfortable talking to Mitch. Their late-night conversations had given them a connection and he was easy to talk to. She didn't mind *talking* about her transplant, she was only reluctant for people to see her toes. Her abdominal scars didn't bother her, they were nothing out of the ordinary, but her disfigured toes were another story.

'So now I have three kidneys. My two useless ones and a new one. So, yes, I do drink a lot of water and when I go to the bathroom sometimes it's to take my immunosuppressant medication. I don't want to take tablets in front of the children.'

Mitch was nodding. Rose knew that most of what she'd told him made sense. It didn't explain her crappy balance but that was a story for another day.

'Your donor? Was it someone in your family?'

'No. My mum and Ruby weren't a match and Scarlett was pregnant at the time and unlikely to be compatible if the others weren't.'

'Why do you say that?'

'We're half-sisters. Same mother but different fathers.'

'What about your father's side of the family?'

'My dad died when I was eight. There is no one else.'

Mitch had limited experience with transplant medicine. He'd been a country doctor and specialised medicine like transplant surgery was always dealt with in the city. He knew some of the theory but was less familiar with the practical side of things, though he knew enough to know that exposure to infection posed a serious risk. 'Surely a hospital is the last place you should be working, given the risk of infection?' The doctor in him, the doctor he tried so hard to forget, couldn't resist asking the question. And, as long as they continued to talk about her, the topic of his past could stay buried, which was just how he liked it.

'I had to be extra careful in the first twelve months after surgery not to get sick. I still need to be careful but it's been eighteen months now. I'm not allowed to work with children who have recently had live vaccines like polio or measles, mumps and rubella, but if the children are infectious they're not allowed into the classroom at all anyway. There are plenty of other patients who can't afford to get an infection—our cystic fibrosis patients, our chemotherapy patients— it's not just me. So it's actually a better environment for me, it's far more controlled than it would be working in a normal primary school where children will turn up after having vaccinations or when they have a cold. And working in the hospital is less tiring.' She smiled. 'There's no yard duty, no early mornings, no late-night parent interviews or concerts, no excursions. It's pretty easy.'

To someone who hadn't spent fifteen years

learning how to read body language, learning to listen for the unspoken worry or to pick up on the seemingly innocuous sign, Rose would seem quite relaxed. As if she'd dealt with her situation, come to terms with it and moved on, but he still sensed that something wasn't quite right. It might not be major but he would bet money there was still something bothering her. This time he wasn't relying on his sixth sense to tell him—Rose was playing with her hair. She was uncomfortable about something.

He was intrigued enough to dig deeper but recognised that it really wasn't any of his business. He didn't need to ask questions. He didn't need to research transplant medicine. His days of practising medicine were finished. And Rose wasn't his patient.

He should forget about it. Forget about her. But he knew that was going to be difficult.

He wished he could remain an impartial spectator but he knew that was impossible. Just like today he had found it difficult to stand by and do nothing. No matter how often he told himself he wasn't a doctor any more, his training couldn't be obliterated entirely and he knew there was more to Rose's story. His sixth sense was working overtime.

He knew he should forget about her, he didn't need to know what was wrong, but he hadn't been able to stop thinking about her. He couldn't get her out of his head and now, more than ever, he knew he would continue to think about her, for all sorts of reasons. The timing wasn't right and neither were the logistics. He was only in Adelaide temporarily and had two young children in tow plus another in hospital. And he was leaving town again tomorrow. He'd be back once more to collect Lila when she was discharged and that was it. It was hardly the right time or place to develop a fascination with a woman and definitely not the time or place to get involved with her.

But that didn't stop him wishing things were different. It had been years since anyone had captured his attention like Rose had and that was proving difficult to ignore. Perhaps his period of mourning was actually over. He hated being alone on the station, and right now he'd give anything for a chance to have a night, even a few hours, alone with Rose.

But there was no point starting something he couldn't finish.

His timing sucked.

CHAPTER SIX

THIS WAS IT.

This was the end.

Lila would be discharged on Monday, which meant Mitch would have no reason to return to Adelaide. Rose wouldn't see him any more. She'd missed her chance.

Not that he'd really given her a chance.

Should she have pushed him? The old Rose wouldn't have hesitated. But the old Rose had been full of confidence. The old Rose had never been rejected. The new Rose wasn't brave enough to make the first move. She was too scared of what would happen next. Too afraid now of physical intimacy. It was too much of a risk for just one night. She wasn't brave enough.

She wasn't ready. But she knew she was going to regret it.

Time had dragged when Mitch was back on the station. The frequent phone calls were no longer enough. She wanted to see him smile. She wanted to touch him.

The past two weeks since he'd headed north again had seemed like an eternity and she had no idea how she was going to survive once he was gone for good.

She hadn't been able to stop thinking about him. Her libido had well and truly come alive again but it was too late.

Maybe she should have taken a chance, she thought as she pulled to a stop in front of the apartment complex where Mitch and the boys were staying again.

What was the worst that could happen? If he rejected her she could live with that. Maybe. At least if she did get rebuffed she wasn't likely to bump into him in the street and be forced to live out her humiliation all over again. Maybe it was a case of now or never. Maybe it was time for her to move forward. Maybe if she got the opportunity she should take it and see what happened.

Maybe she should be brave.

Mitch had asked if she could do him a favour and look after the boys for a couple of hours while he attended some meetings. She'd agreed without hesitation, not even bothering to find out what the meetings were. It didn't matter.

All that mattered was having another chance to see him again.

'Hi,' he greeted her with a kiss on the cheek and Rose bit back her disappointment. Was that all their relationship was ever going to be now? A platonic kiss on the cheek? Had she really missed her chance to experience him? 'Thanks so much for doing this,' he said as he stepped back to let her into the apartment.

'It's a pleasure,' she said as the boys came running out of their bedroom to greet her. Charlie had his arms in the air, imploring her to pick him up, and she was happy to oblige. She lifted him onto her hip and hugged him tight, loving the way his little soft body felt in her arms. She blinked back tears. What was the matter with her?

She knew what it was. Unresolved desire. Her hormones were driving her crazy.

'I thought I'd take the boys down to the River Torrens, we might go for a boat ride on *Popeye,* depending on how long you'll be,' she said.

'I'll be a couple of hours. I hope that's okay? I have appointments to interview new governesses. In all the drama with Lila and all the backwards and forwards to town I'd completely forgotten that Ginny is about to go off backpacking around Europe. She advertised for a replacement from up our way but there hasn't been anyone suitable so she's set up some interviews down here. I'll call you as soon as I'm done and meet you in town.'

Rose gathered the boys and the backpack Mitch had filled for her with spare clothes, drink bottles and snacks.

She enjoyed spending time with Mitch's boys. It was almost as good as spending time with him but even so she was more than happy to see his smiling face when he arrived at the river bank.

'How did the interviews go?' she asked, as she handed him a packet of biscuits in exchange for a hot chocolate he had brought for her.

'Not great,' he sighed as he sat on the bench beside her. 'I had hoped that *one* of the three might have been okay. I'd hoped I'd be able to introduce them to the kids and then offer them the position and have it all sorted by the time we leave on Monday, but I'm back to square one.'

'What was wrong with them?'

Mitch chewed his biscuit and watched the boys throw bread to the ducks while he deliberated over his answer. 'I know one wouldn't cope with being stuck out in the middle of nowhere, she was far too high maintenance *and* a vegetarian. Can you imagine, on a cattle station? Some days we have red meat with every meal.'

'Maybe she was just trying to make a good impression.'

Mitch laughed. 'Well, that wasn't the way to go about it. The second one was a German tourist; she's studying to be a teacher but her visa means she can only work in a job for three months before having to move. I don't want to go through this all again in a couple of months' time.'

'Why did you even interview her?'

'I'm desperate. Ginny leaves in two weeks.'

'And the third one?'

'She was an older lady who was very old school. My kids are young and busy and they need to have fun still. I realise they need schooling but there are sports camps, rodeos, swimming in the creek when we have water, and I just can't see Mrs Abbott doing any of that.'

'And there was no one from up your way?'

Mitch shook his head. 'No. It's really difficult at this time of year. Governesses have been in their positions for less than a term, it's too soon for them to decide they don't fit with the family and want to move on and I can't manage without anyone. It's not just the schooling, it wouldn't matter if they missed a few weeks of that, but I'm going to need someone who can drive Lila to town for her appointments and rehab. Those trips will need overnight stays; I can't keep leav-

ing the station and I can't always take the boys.
Our staff numbers are low, I've had to let a lot
of casual staff go because of the drought, and
I really don't have the spare manpower. I'm already stretched thin.'

'Do you think I could do it?' Rose couldn't
resist offering to help. She'd been mulling over
the idea ever since Mitch had told her what was
happening that morning. In her mind she'd come
up with the perfect solution. Mitch needed help,
help she was qualified to offer, and she wouldn't
have to say goodbye. To him or the kids. She'd
grown attached to Lila and the boys and she
didn't want anyone else taking what she already
pictured as her place.

'You?'

She nodded. 'It's what I'm trained to do.' Her
voice was eager as she tried to convince Mitch
that her idea made sense. 'If I can manage a
classroom of nine-year-olds I think I can manage your three.' She couldn't physically manage
a classroom of nine-year-olds, which was one
of the reasons why the low-key hospital teaching job suited her, but she didn't share that information. 'I could come out there. Just for a
few months,' she added, as she didn't want to
seem too pushy. 'It would give you some breathing space, some time to find someone else. I'm

qualified. I'm not a vegetarian. I can help with Lila and the kids already know me.'

'But you have a job.'

'I'm actually only on contract covering someone's maternity leave. She's due back at work next term and I've applied for another contract but that will depend on whether or not there's work. I won't be letting anyone down,' she insisted. 'I could do this.'

Please, say yes, she thought.

'Do you realise what it would be like? It's not a Monday to Friday job. There're not too many places to go when you knock off for the day. Actually, there's nowhere to go. We're five hours from the nearest town. You'll spend days and days on the station surrounded by the same people, eating together, socialising together, and even if you're not with the children they'll never be far away. You don't get to go home to your own space.'

It didn't sound very different to her life now. She didn't go out much any more; she'd probably have more company on the station than she had in the city. She didn't need the bright city lights. What she needed was room to breathe. Space. And Mitch would be there. She thought the station would be perfect.

'It's nothing like you might imagine, Rose,' Mitch continued. 'I don't know what you've seen on television but the reality is very different from the movies. There's a reason that movies depicting the end of the world or a desolate future civilisation are shot out my way. We haven't had rain for three years, it's a huge red dust bowl. It's stinking hot and the flies will drive you crazy.'

'But yet you're still there.' Rose smiled. 'There have to be some redeeming features.'

There were plenty of redeeming features but Mitch wasn't sure a city girl would see them in quite the same light. Lord knew, there'd been plenty of times in the past two years when he would have happily chucked it all in, redeeming features or not, but he'd kept going.

'It's my home. It's my kids' home.'

The station belonged to his children; they would inherit it, and he was just the custodian, but he owed it to them to keep it going. There were plenty of times when he could have happily given it away—it wouldn't fetch much if he tried to sell it, not in the current market—but it wasn't in his nature to give up and he did love it. He could cope with the stress caused by Mother Nature, he was used to the stress of life on a cattle station and that was preferable to the stress of moving to town.

Besides, what would he do then? The Outback got under your skin, into your blood, and he couldn't really imagine leaving for ever, but a break every now and then would be nice. Just to have the opportunity to get away, to recharge his batteries. Perhaps if he had someone to share his life with he wouldn't feel so pressured. Having someone else to help shoulder the burden would make a difference. But that wasn't a governess's role.

But Rose didn't need to know all that. The Outback was no place for her.

'What about your health? We're out in the middle of nowhere.'

'I'm perfectly stable. As long as I have my medication there's no problem. You're so isolated I imagine there's less chance of me picking up an infection out there than in town. But if you don't want me there, just tell me.'

But he *did* want her there. That was the problem. He could imagine sitting down at the end of the day and sharing a drink with her on the veranda. She was easy company and gorgeous, and therein lay the problem. He was attracted to her but he didn't want to risk bringing her out to the station. But that begged the question of *why* he felt like that. What was at stake?

He knew he was worried he might do something he'd regret. He might find temptation too strong. It wasn't that he intended to stay celibate for the rest of his life—he hadn't considered himself celibate at all—but he was planning on staying single and he didn't think Rose was the type of girl he should fool around with. She was only twenty-three, still young, just out of teacher's college, just a girl really compared to him. He was thirty-nine, jaded and weary. It would be completely inappropriate.

'All I'm asking you to do is think about it,' Rose said. 'Think about what other options you've got and get back to me.'

'Okay,' he agreed. Would it really be so terrible just to consider her offer? He knew he'd like to have her company but he wasn't sure if offering her the job was the sensible thing to do. In fact, he was pretty certain it wasn't at all sensible. But for purely selfish reasons he would consider it.

He'd agreed to think about it! Rose crossed her fingers in her lap. She was counting on the fact he didn't have any other options. They both knew that. She had decided it was time to be brave, and this was her being brave.

Plus, she thought it sounded so romantic, living on a remote cattle station. She could imagine herself in riding boots and a stockman's hat. Not actually on a horse as she didn't know how to ride, but she liked the outfit. She'd plant a vegetable garden with the children and teach them about the wide world. Not that she'd travelled far.

Was she crazy, trying to convince Mitch to hire her? He was right, she didn't know the first thing about living in a remote place.

But she did know about children. And whatever else she didn't know, she'd learn.

'The boys are asleep,' Rose said as she returned to the living room after reading them a bedtime story.

He'd invited her to stay for dinner. It was just a takeaway but this was likely to be the last night he'd have the pleasure of her company. Once he took Lila home that would be it. Unless he offered Rose the job she wanted. But that wasn't going to happen. That would be madness.

He handed her the small glass of wine that was still half-full.

She hitched her dress up above her knees as she tucked one leg under her and sat on the couch beside him. The apartment was small and sparsely furnished, and there wasn't really anywhere else to sit but tonight Mitch was very aware of how close she was. He hadn't seen her in a dress before. It was made out of stretchy cotton, nothing fancy, but it hugged her slight curves and showed off her smooth, toned legs.

She sipped her wine and leant forward, placing it on the coffee table. He could feel her body heat, smell her perfume. She smelt like roses.

Her dress pulled tight across her chest as she leant forward, drawing his eyes to her breasts. They were small and pert, perfectly shaped, and her nipples were erect, jutting against the soft cotton of her dress.

He felt his body respond. He shifted slightly in his seat as his erection started to grow, pushing against the fabric of his shorts.

They'd shared a bottle of wine tonight but Rose was still on her first glass. Maybe his inhibitions had been dampened by the alcohol. That might not have been his smartest idea but he hadn't really expected Rose to accept his offer of wine as she normally refused alcohol.

Was she aware of him too? Had the half-glass of wine she'd drunk relaxed her?

She was close enough to touch and he was thinking about doing just that, thinking about how she would feel, when he felt her hand on his thigh. Her hand was warm and small and her last two fingers were below the hem of his shorts so he could feel the heat on his skin.

She was still leaning towards him. His senses were overloaded. The smell of her rose-scented perfume, the touch of her hand on his leg, the sight of her lips, pink and full. He couldn't keep his eyes off them and he wondered how she would taste. Her lips were moving and that was when he realised she was speaking to him. She was saying something and it took all of his concentration to listen and understand what she was saying.

'There's something I need to do. Just in case you leave on Monday without me.'

She was closer still. There were only centimetres separating them and suddenly the distance was nothing at all.

She was kissing him. Her lips were pressed against his, slightly parted, and they were warm and soft, softer than he'd imagined.

She tasted of strawberries.

That was unexpected.

Everything was unexpected but not unpleasant.

Mitch could feel his body responding. His reaction was immediate and while it was completely understandable it was also completely out of his control.

He hadn't been a monk since Cara had died but it had been months since he'd been with a woman. It wasn't easy on the station. He didn't get a lot of time or opportunity and here was Rose presenting him with opportunity. He wasn't about to argue.

But he had his own idea of how this was going to go.

He took control, deepening the kiss. His tongue parted her lips and her mouth opened under his.

He wrapped his left hand around her hips, pulling her closer. He slid his right hand behind her neck, through the silken strands of her hair as he held her to him. Ever since he'd first laid eyes on her he'd wanted to feel her hair around his fingers but all that was forgotten now. There was so much more to feel. So much more to experience.

He moved his left hand and ran it underneath the hem of her dress, pushing it higher as his hand spanned the inside of her thigh.

Rose moaned and spread her knees, twisting so that now she sat astride his lap. He could feel his erection pressing into her, nestled in the junction of her thighs. His heart rate was rapid, working hard to pump the blood through his arteries. His groin throbbed, engorged and swollen.

Her fingers were at his throat, running down to where his collarbones met and then further, teasing open the top button of his shirt and then the next. Her palms were spread flat on his chest. Two matching circles of heat, one resting over his frantically beating heart.

His hand was under her dress and he pressed his fingers over the soft mound between her thighs. Rose moaned and pushed towards him as he cupped her. His fingers pushed aside the fabric of her underwear and slid inside her. She was warm and wet and Mitch wanted to take her right then and there. He wanted to tear her underwear off and bury himself inside her. He could imagine how it would feel to be deep inside her, to have her long, smooth legs wrapped around his waist as he thrust into her.

His thumb circled her clitoris as she arched her back.

He pushed her dress higher and felt the smooth skin of her back under his palm. He traced her rib cage and his fingers spanned her side. He moved his hand further until he could cup her breast and then ran his thumb over her nipple and felt it peak through the fabric of her bra. He pushed the cup aside and took her breast into his mouth. His tongue rolled over her nipple, sucking it and pulling it gently as she moaned and ground herself against his hand.

Her clitoris was swollen, a tight little nub under his fingers, as she spread her legs further, encouraging him deeper inside her.

'Oh, God, Mitch, I don't think I can wait.'

He wanted to bury himself inside her but he had no protection. There would be time for him later. He wanted to give her this. He lifted his head from her breast. 'I want you to come now.'

He watched her give in to the pleasure.

Her eyelids were heavy over her green eyes. Her lips were parted and her tongue darted out between her lips as she panted. She took a deep breath and he saw her breasts rise and fall as she writhed in his lap.

Her eyelids closed as she took another deep breath. This one she held and he could tell she'd forgotten to breathe out. All her energy, all her focus, was centred on pleasure.

He knew she was close now and his fingers worked a bit faster.

He watched her as she came. She cried out and he felt her shudder. Felt her muscles tense around his fingers and felt her relax once she was spent. She came to rest, her weight on his chest and in his lap. She felt good. Warm and slick against his skin. He could have stayed like that for a long time but he had other plans for her.

'Sorry, I couldn't stop,' she said, her voice muffled against his chest.

'Don't apologise. The night's not over yet.'

He wrapped his arms around her and was about to lift her up and carry her to his room when he heard a second voice.

'Daddy?'

Rose pulled back as if someone had yanked her away from him and slid off his lap. Her luminous green eyes were wide, her pupils dilated. He wasn't sure whether that was due to fright or desire. Probably a bit of both now.

Mitch looked to his right, half expecting to see Charlie standing in the doorway, but he was nowhere to be seen.

'I'm thirsty.'

Mitch breathed a sigh of relief. Charlie was still in his bed, calling out from his room.

What had he been thinking, seducing Rose while his children slept in the next room?

He hadn't been thinking. His mind had been completely consumed by Rose and he'd forgotten about his children.

Rose tugged her dress down to restore her modesty, although it was a little too late for that. She could feel her face growing hot as a blush spread over her cheeks. Thank goodness Charlie hadn't got out of bed. She would have been mortified if he'd surprised them on the couch.

Mitch was looking to his right, his thoughts clearly on his kids.

She sensed he was feeling uncomfortable. Awkward. Probably a little bit guilty. All the same feelings she was experiencing.

'I'd better go,' she said.

She knew his children were his first priority, despite what had just happened between them.

She was actually a little bit relieved that Charlie had woken up. The kiss had escalated much faster than she'd anticipated and if they hadn't been interrupted she knew she would have found herself in a predicament—wanting to make love to Mitch but not wanting to get naked. She'd need to work through that. It might be that she and Mitch would never get another chance but all the same it was a problem that needed a solution. Maybe not tonight, and maybe not with Mitch, but at some point in the future it was a bridge she'd have to cross.

'Will you still think about giving me the job?' she asked as he stood up.

'Was that what the kiss was about? The job?'

'No! I didn't kiss you to make you see my point of view. I kissed you because I wanted to. Because I was afraid that if I didn't I might miss my chance.' Rose was pleased she'd been brave enough to take the chance. The kiss had been everything she'd hoped for and even if she didn't get what she wanted in the end, even if she didn't get to go back to the station with him, at least she knew what it was like to kiss him. 'I didn't really expect it to end like that, not that I'm complaining, but now we both know we want more I really think you should give me a chance. I think you should take me home with you.'

'I can't.'

Mitch walked over to the kitchen sink and washed his hands before getting a cup and filling it with water for Charlie. There was no discussion. Just an abrupt two words.

Rose followed him. She had plucked up her courage once tonight, desperate to make the most of what might have been her only chance, but now she couldn't let it go. 'I'm not asking for forever. Just a few months. You can ignore the chemistry between us if you like but I don't have a permanent job and you need a governess. This could be good for both of us. Won't you think about it some more?'

'I didn't say I won't, I said I can't. I can't keep you safe. I live in the middle of the country, in the middle of nowhere. If something goes wrong we are hundreds of miles and several hours from even basic medical care.'

'But you're a doctor. Surely that counts for something?'

'I'm not a doctor any more. I don't want that responsibility. There's enough resting on my shoulders without willingly taking on more risk.'

She'd been desperate for an opportunity to ask him more about his past, about why he'd given medicine away, but she got the distinct impression that the topic was off limits.

'But I'm perfectly fine,' she argued. 'Surely you can see that.' When he didn't answer she added, 'What if I get medical clearance from my own doctor? Then I'm not your responsibility any more.'

'You'd still be my responsibility, everyone on the station is.'

'But I haven't even had a cold for almost a year. Scarlett can back me up, she's a doctor too. Why don't I arrange a meeting for you? I give you permission to discuss my health with her, but if she has no reservations will you at least agree to think about it? I'll speak to Scarlett and see if we can meet her tomorrow. Please?'

Mitch nodded and prepared himself to say goodbye. He would go with her to speak to Scarlett but he knew he was only agreeing so that he didn't feel like a complete heel. He couldn't just say goodbye and return to the station. Not after what had just transpired between them. That would be the equivalent of promising to call and not ringing. If he didn't acquiesce to her request he'd feel he'd taken advantage of her. So, to assuage his guilt, he agreed.

* * *

The guilt was still with him as he pulled up in front of Scarlett's house the next morning.

Guilt over what had happened and over where. He still couldn't believe he'd forgotten about his children sleeping in the next room. If Charlie hadn't woken up he would have carried Rose to his bed and made love to her. He hadn't planned it but neither of them had looked remotely capable of putting a stop to proceedings and he knew he hadn't wanted to.

He hadn't been celibate since Cara had died but none of them had elicited the reaction that Rose did. With the others he would have been able to stop.

He could walk away from them; in fact, he'd done just that. Slept with them once and once only. But something told him that once with Rose wouldn't be enough. Perhaps it was fortunate that Charlie had interrupted them. Perhaps it was for the best. He wasn't going to take Rose back to the station. He'd meant it when he'd said he didn't want the responsibility. He wasn't taking her with him and he didn't want to make it any harder to walk away. Which brought him back to the reason he was here. Guilt. He felt like he'd taken advantage of Rose, although rationally he knew that wasn't really the case.

Scarlett greeted them at the door. Rose had

told him that her brother-in-law Jake would be at work. That was good, one less person to deal with.

Scarlett was not what he'd been expecting. He knew they were half-sisters but he'd still just envisaged a slightly older version of Rose, but Scarlett was dark where Rose was fair and she was shorter and much curvier than her younger sister. The far bigger surprise was her two-year-old daughter who was perched on her hip.

He'd forgotten about Holly.

He hoped he managed to hide his apprehension as Scarlett welcomed them into her home.

Holly was a month or two older than his own daughter would have been and that was much too close for comfort. Holly was dark haired like her mother and like he always imagined his daughter would have been. Dark like Lila. The familiar ache was back in his heart. He hadn't been aware of it much lately, he'd learnt to compartmentalise his pain and he usually managed to avoid babies. It wasn't difficult on the station, but there was no way to avoid Holly.

But luckily Holly wasn't interested in him. Her eyes went straight to Jed and Charlie, who followed in his shadow. Potential playmates.

Scarlett led them out to a small back garden. There was a sandpit in one corner and the boys were more than happy to play there with Holly.

Mitch was free to ignore her but, no matter how much he wanted to, he found his eyes drawn to the sand pit. That could have been Jed and Charlie with their own little sister.

Scarlett offered him and Rose a drink. While she went to make tea Mitch turned his chair, adjusting it so he couldn't easily see the children. It was too difficult to watch.

When Scarlett returned, Rose took her mug and went to sit with the children, leaving Scarlett and Mitch free to talk.

'Rose told me she's applied for a governess position on your station?'

Scarlett's tone seemed to imply she thought he might be encouraging the whole idea. 'Yes…' He drew the word out, not quite sure what she wanted to hear from him.

'She also mentioned you weren't keen on the idea?'

'That's right.'

'But she seems to think that you're being a bit cautious and wants me to plead her case.'

'So she said.'

'Rose said you're worried about her health.' Mitch nodded.

'She also told me you're a qualified doctor?' Mitch nodded again.

'So you would know the risks.'

'I do. And that's exactly the problem. I realise

from Rose's point of view the worst that would happen would be that she would contract an infection. She figures there would be no great emergency, that we'd call the flying doctor and get her some antibiotics or evacuate her. But the flying doctor can't always get through.'

'Surely they would get to you in a time. She's right, it's hardly likely to be an emergency. Rose also told me you have a pilot and a plane. Would it be so difficult to evacuate her yourself?'

'Assuming there are no other unforeseen problems or natural disasters, no, it wouldn't, but our airstrip has been out of action from flooding at times.'

'Are you expecting rain? Rose told me it hasn't rained for three years.'

Mitch shook his head. 'No,' he admitted. 'The rains generally come in summer. We'll probably have to wait another year. I know there's probably only a low risk associated with Rose being out there but a low risk is still too high in my opinion. I don't want to be responsible for her. I don't want to have to worry about keeping her safe.'

Despite telling himself Rose's transplant was none of his business, he hadn't been able to stop himself from doing some research and getting up to speed on the implications of her surgery. He still had an inquisitive medical brain even if he didn't want to practise medicine, and he could tell that Scarlett couldn't quite understand why he was protesting so much. She was right, the risk really was small enough to be managed. Unless something unforeseen happened. And he couldn't risk that. 'I *know* things can go wrong when you least expect them to and, out there, any mistake is magnified. I've been through it before.' He paused and took a breath. 'My wife died on that station.'

'I'm so sorry. Rose didn't tell me.'

Mitch shook his head. 'Rose doesn't know the details.' He picked up his drink. He wasn't thirsty but it gave him time to think about how much to tell her. 'My wife was pregnant. I lost her and the baby. There was nothing I could do.' He lifted a hand, rubbing it over his face in an attempt to wipe the memory away. 'I'm worried that if Rose falls ill we might actually be too far from medical help. There's only so much I can do on my own.'

She understood. He could see it in her eyes.

'I didn't think you'd be advocating for this move anyway,' he said. Rose had mentioned Scarlett's protective tendencies. He couldn't imagine she would think Rose was making a wise decision. Rose wasn't a seasoned traveller or particularly adventurous. Moving to the middle of nowhere with a stranger wouldn't be the kind of thing her family would expect of her. It sounded more like something their other sister, Ruby, would do.

'I'm not,' Scarlett replied. 'But it wasn't because of Rose's health. I have other concerns.'

'Such as?'

'Her heart, not her health.'

'Meaning?'

'I don't want her to get hurt. I think she's looking at life on a station, and at you, through rose-coloured glasses. That saying is perfectly suited to her, it could have been written about her. I don't know how she manages to but she still believes in happy endings, despite everything that has happened to her. Her father died when she was young, then she got so sick. She still believes in true love. She thinks that will solve the world's problems. And her own. But I don't think she's likely to find true love in the middle of the Outback. She needs to stay in the city, not because of her health but because she needs to get out and about, she needs to meet people, to get on with her life. I don't mean to sound rude, but do you really think that living on a station in the middle of nowhere with a widower and his three kids is the best environment for her? Unless there's something going on between the two of you that I don't know about?' She raised an eyebrow and looked at him.

Thank goodness he didn't get embarrassed easily, Mitch thought. He knew his tanned, olive skin would hide any tell-tale signs of embarrassment. If Rose hadn't found it necessary to tell her sister what had transpired last night, he certainly wasn't going to. But despite his discomfiture he found Scarlett amusing. She called a spade a spade and so did he but he didn't like being questioned or told what to do and the more Scarlett tried to push him away from Rose the more he found himself thinking of all the reasons why he should take her home with him.

'So, how did that go?' Rose asked as they drove away.

'Better than I expected.'

'Meaning she agrees with you.'

'Not exactly. But she did help me to clarify a few things.'

'Like what?'

'Like why you would be perfect for the job.'

'Really?'

Mitch nodded, knowing he wasn't thinking with his head or his heart but with other parts of his anatomy. Yet, even knowing that, he was unable to stop himself from offering her the position. He knew that once he took Lila home from hospital there would be no reason to see

Rose any more and he couldn't imagine saying goodbye. Not after last night.

But it was more than that. She'd been a breath of fresh air, she'd been something to look forward to, and he hadn't felt that in a long time. He knew he shouldn't be mixing business and pleasure and he should *definitely* not be entertaining thoughts of sleeping with the governess, but he couldn't imagine letting her go.

There were two very good reasons why he should offer her the job and only one reason why he shouldn't. Rose was right. He needed someone to help with the children and he enjoyed her company. He could have his cake and eat it too. And maybe Rose was also right about the station being a less risky environment in terms of exposure to bugs. There was a chance she'd be less exposed to common viruses being away from large populations of people. He knew he was talking himself into it because it was what he wanted but did that make it wrong? If it was what they both wanted, then surely that made it okay.

'I need help with the children and I've seen how good you are with them. You've even got Lila talking again. The job is yours if you want it.'

CHAPTER SEVEN

'THERE SHE IS.'

The pilot's voice came through Rose's headset and, as he banked the small plane to the right, Rose caught her first glimpse of Emu Downs.

She'd been looking out the window intermittently ever since Steve had taken off from Broken Hill but the landscape had been a fairly uniform shade of dusty ochre with the occasional dry river bed and some scrubby green-grey vegetation. Now she could pick out some small buildings, their silver corrugated tin roofs glinting in the sunlight. There were more buildings than she'd expected, a dozen at least, giving the impression of a small village and one long roof had 'EMU DOWNS' painted on it in large black letters.

Rose had seen one mob of emus running across the sand as the plane had travelled northeast, the birds' shadows stretching across the red dirt larger than they were. The sight had made her smile. Mitch might have said that the emu numbers were depleted but Rose was happy to have seen some. It made it feel real.

Her heart was in her mouth as the pilot banked. She was almost there and Mitch would be waiting.

As the plane dropped lower in the sky she could see movement. Dust rose from the tyres of moving vehicles and swirled around smaller, dark brown shapes that morphed into cattle.

This was it. She'd arrived.

The ground disappeared beneath the plane and Rose's teeth snapped together in her jaw as the wheels bumped on the dirt runway. Steve turned the plane in a tight circle and Rose watched as the wingtip passed over the thin wire strands of a fence before they straightened up and taxied to a halt next to a four-wheel drive.

Through the small windows of the plane she could see Mitch and the children waiting by the vehicle. The children were waving and Rose waved back but she was looking at Mitch. It had only been three weeks since she'd seen him but she'd almost forgotten how handsome he was.

She caught her breath. She'd been imagining this arrival for days and she could scarcely believe she was finally here.

Steve reached across her lap and unlocked the

small door beside her. Rose unclipped her seat belt and clambered out. Eager to get to Mitch.

'Welcome to Emu Downs.' He was standing behind the children. She expected him to come forward, she wanted to step into his arms, but he stayed where he was, barricaded behind the kids, shielded from her.

He extended his hand. Such a formal greeting surprised her. She was completely taken aback. What was going on? But as she shook his hand and he smiled at her some of her reservations receded slightly. His smile was as warm and friendly as she remembered. Perhaps she couldn't expect a big display of affection in front of the children. That probably wasn't appropriate given that she was now employed as their governess. Perhaps when they were alone things would be different.

She smiled back and reminded herself to ask Mitch what the ground rules were going to be. That was probably something they should have discussed but the whole exercise had happened in such a rush and, admittedly, she hadn't thought rules were too important.

The kids gathered around her as she let go of Mitch's hand. Jed and Lila hugged her and Charlie raised his arms, requesting to be lifted up. At least the kids didn't have reservations.

'How was your trip?'

'Long,' she replied. 'You weren't kidding when you said you're in the middle of nowhere.' She'd caught a bus from Adelaide to Broken Hill and then Steve had collected her from there. Flying into Emu Downs had shaved hours off a dusty, bumpy trip but she'd still been travelling for most of the day.

Another man, about her age, with brown skin and black eyes and a friendly expression, came around from behind the four-wheel drive. She hadn't noticed him until he'd moved. She'd only had eyes for Mitch.

'Rose, this is Jimmy. Jimmy, Rose,' Mitch said as he picked up her bags and stashed them into the back of the four-wheel drive. 'You'll need to get to know Jimmy, he'll be teaching you how to ride.'

Jimmy smiled at her as he closed the cargo door and his teeth flashed white against his dark skin. He ducked his head in acknowledgement but didn't speak.

'You're just in time for afternoon smoko. Jimmy will take your bags to your accommodation and if you're up for it we'll grab a cuppa and you can meet everyone.'

Rose was exhausted but she didn't want to miss a minute of the whole experience. She would have loved a shower but she could do that later. Smoko meant everyone would be in one place and it would be easiest to meet them all now. Best to get it over and done with.

Mitch introduced her to Shirley first. 'Shirley is our cook,' he said. 'She's the most important person here.'

'You have some things in your room, your accommodation has a kitchen,' Shirley told her as she showed her where the tea and coffee were kept, 'but meals are served here and shared together. We're isolated enough without people eating their meals alone.'

Rose took a tea bag and mug from the shelf. On the table behind her was an assortment of food; a large carrot cake, fresh scones, fruit and biscuits.

'Do you have any allergies I need to know about?' Shirley asked as Rose added boiling water to her tea.

'I can't eat some raw foods but I can control that. I don't have any allergies,' she replied.

'So I take it you're okay with red meat?' Shirley was grinning and Rose smiled back.

'Definitely.'

Mitch introduced her to the rest of the staff while she devoured a scone and a piece of cake. She'd have to watch what she ate if all Shirley's cooking was this good.

'We'll finish the tour and then I'll let you get settled,' Mitch said as Rose drained the last of her tea. 'You'd probably like a shower but one word of advice, most of us will shower at the end of the day. It's so dusty out here there's not much point showering until you're almost ready for bed. Saves getting covered in dust all over again,' he said as they walked away from the kitchen and up a slight hill.

Rose knew water was scarce on the station but his comment just made her think about showering with Mitch—she could do her bit for water conservation that way. Mitch was still talking and she forced herself to concentrate on what he was telling her.

'This is the original house,' he was saying. 'When we built the new house…' he pointed to a second dwelling about twenty metres away '…we turned this into the school house but kept living quarters for the governess. It's more comfortable than the workers' accommodation. I think you'll prefer it here.'

He pushed open the front door and they stepped inside. It was built out of wood in the typical Queensland style, with a wide veranda and elevated off the ground to let the breeze through and stop it from drowning in a flood. There were four rooms off the hallway, two either side. The first two, left and right of the front door, had been kept as a bedroom and a living room but the next two had been knocked through and converted into one long room that ran the width of the house and was now the school room. Bookshelves and pin boards lined the walls and there were a couple of large tables in the centre that served as desks. Two laptop computers sat on a third table in the corner. A kitchen, laundry and bathroom were at the back of the house.

Rose wandered through the rooms. 'This is fabulous,' she said. 'The school room looks a much better set-up than I'd imagined.' She'd brought a whole suitcase on the plane with her that was packed with textbooks, novels and early readers as well as pencils and craft supplies. She hadn't known what to expect and was surprised by the number of resources that appeared to be at her disposal.

She stuck her head into her bedroom. The room was furnished with a pine dresser and wardrobe, a double bed, made up with pretty white linen, and soft sheer curtains framed the windows and French doors. She had her own space, which was perfect, and from her front veranda she could look across a rather dry and desolate flower garden to the main house and what she assumed was Mitch's veranda.

Two old armchairs sat on the wooden boards looking out across the river bed. It was dry and stony, completely devoid of water, but despite the barrenness of the land, the red dirt and the dust, it had a certain beauty. A sense of calm. She could just imagine sitting out there in the evening, chatting to Mitch about their days.

'Sorry, what was that?'

'I was going to take you around the rest of the buildings if you're not too tired. And then you can unpack and rest when I go back to work.'

'Sure.'

The children accompanied them as Mitch showed her the set-up. Along with the airstrip, the main house and the school house there was also a kitchen block, where she'd had smoko, a recreation room for the staff, staff quarters for the single workers, a couple of small houses for the married staff and multiple sheds plus the stables, veggie garden, chook pen and the cattle yards. It was like a small country town.

'This is not at all what I expected,' she said.

'Better or worse?'

'Better, I think.' The facilities were definitely better than she'd imagined but Mitch was different. He wasn't as relaxed. More stressed. Was he nervous? She couldn't imagine so but he seemed on edge. He wasn't quite meeting her eyes and a couple of times he'd stepped away if she got too close. She hated to admit it but it bothered her. She wanted to feel comfortable, she wanted *him* to feel comfortable, with his decision to have her there. But maybe she was being too sensitive, maybe it had nothing to do with her. Maybe there was something on his mind that she knew nothing about.

Time would tell. She wouldn't worry about it now. They both had some adjusting to do.

The first few days passed in a blur as Rose got used to her new surroundings and settled into station life. It was foreign, hot, dusty and dry but it had a certain beauty to it all and she remembered Mitch's description. He had summed it up perfectly. The clear air and the bright, crisp colours were like nothing she'd ever seen before. It was beautiful but what he hadn't described was the silence. It was enormous, particularly at dawn and twilight when it was only broken by the sound of the wildlife—the birds, the crickets and the frogs—and she found it surprisingly comforting.

But her absolute favourite time of day was the early morning. She loved the freshness and the breath of possibility that came with each new day and she found herself believing in good things again. There was no room for melancholy thoughts in her head, she was surrounded by too much beauty.

The job was demanding but exciting and her days were busy but not difficult. The role of a governess was new to her and she was having to learn fast, but she was coping. She had to get up to speed with the School of the Air, what was expected of her and what stages the children were at but that was the easy part. That was the teaching part. It was the rest of the governess's role that was challenging. Her teaching degree couldn't have prepared her for all the other associated duties that seemed to be part of her job description, including taking charge of Lila's rehabilitation, doing the laundry and getting the children ready for bed, but, like everything, once she got into a routine she felt she had more control.

She spent the morning in the classroom with the children but with just three students, and Charlie only in kindergarten, it didn't take long to get through the work assigned. Which left their afternoons free for all the extra-curricular activities that were on offer. So far they'd cooked with Shirley, been yabbying—unsuccessfully—in the few remaining waterholes and ridden the horses. Lila wasn't anywhere close to getting back on Fudge but she was quite content to spend time at the stable, grooming her. Jimmy, the young jackaroo who Rose had met at the airstrip, had started giving her riding lessons and she absolutely loved it. The exercise, along with the aching muscles, reminded her of when she could run and after just a few days she was sure she could feel an improvement in her strength and stamina. The endorphins that exercise released also helped to brighten her mood.

She fell into bed exhausted each night, as much from the fresh air as from the work. It was a good fatigue, physical rather than mental, as even though her day was long it didn't feel like work. Mitch had warned her about the long days, but she was enjoying spending time with the children and getting to know the other staff and she was almost too busy to notice that she wasn't seeing a lot of Mitch. *Almost* too busy.

She'd expected a bit more communication. A bit more of everything really—more time, more conversation, more flirting, more stolen kisses. She wasn't sure if he was ignoring her or trying to work out how she fitted into things here. Maybe he thought she didn't.

And they were never alone. There always seemed to be someone else nearby, whether by accident or design, Rose wasn't sure.

He was also leaving the children completely to her, which was not what she'd expected. After dinner he disappeared to his study. He'd told her he spent the evenings doing bookwork but somehow she'd imagined things differently and even though she could see his house from hers, they were separated by a dry and dusty flower bed and the distance it created resembled the Great Australian Bight.

From her house she could see him, late in the evening after finishing in his study, sitting alone on his veranda. In her mind he'd looked lonely but possibly he was quite content. He certainly didn't ask for company, not hers definitely.

He didn't seem to have much down time and he certainly didn't spend it with the children. In Rose's opinion that needed to change. The staff all had their jobs to do, and hers was to help raise the children, but they needed their father. They only had one parent, and Rose knew he needed to step up but she hadn't yet worked out how to raise the subject with him. Baby steps, maybe. She needed to establish her role first but in order to do that she needed some guidance from Mitch and that was difficult when he seemed to be doing his best to keep out of her way.

The only time she could guarantee seeing him was at mealtimes. The family ate their meals with the staff, something Rose was taking a little bit of time to get used to, as it all seemed very informal. She never got time alone with Mitch but neither, it seemed, did the children.

On her fifth day he was in the kitchen building and seated for dinner before her. This was her chance. She had questions that needed answering.

She took her plate and sat at the same table. 'Hi.'

'Hello.' He smiled at her. The moment he smiled she almost forgot her concerns. His smile lit a fire inside her and had the power to make her believe that everything was okay. Although in reality she knew it wasn't. 'How are you settling in? Is there anything you need?'

Yes, some time with you.

But being so blunt probably wasn't the way to get what she wanted. 'Actually, there are a few things I need to discuss with you. Can we catch up after I get the children into bed?'

'I've got a pile of bookwork to do.'

She wasn't going to let him ignore her for ever. 'It won't take long. It's important.' She wasn't going to let him put her off. She'd made up her mind to confront him and she intended to do just that. She didn't mind if he thought she needed to discuss the children or their schooling. That was one way to get his attention and if she was being a little sneaky she didn't care. She was getting worried and she needed to know whether he thought it had been a mistake to bring her out here. 'Why don't I come across at eight? Could you take a break then?'

'Okay.'

* * *

Rose got the children to bed and went back to her house to shower. Like everyone else on the station she'd got into the habit of showering at the end of the day to wash the dust away. She wrapped a towel around her body and walked through the house. She flicked through her clothes, looking for something to wear. She spent her days in jeans and riding boots and wanted a change, although she had to admit that as far as footwear went the boots were becoming quite comfortable as the leather softened and because everyone wore them she didn't look out of place. In riding boots her feet looked just the same as everyone else's.

The night was warm. She pulled a pair of shorts from a drawer. She would like to wear a dress as a reminder of what had happened before but she wasn't sure where she stood. Scarlett had warned her, but she hadn't been able to stop herself from getting her hopes up. So far, Mitch hadn't put a foot out of place. He'd been the complete gentleman, a model of propriety, and this wasn't an occasion to get dressed up for.

She wasn't his date; she wasn't his guest. She was his employee.

Had that one night been an aberration? Was

it never going to be repeated? She really needed to know.

She looked out the side window, which looked directly at Mitch's house. She could see the light on in his study. The houses were only metres apart, separated by the narrow garden with the dry and dusty flower beds. She often wondered if the flower beds were a victim of the drought or of Mitch's wife's death. Had she been a keen gardener, had she tended to those beds or had they perished long ago from a lack of water and attention?

Sometimes Rose felt like that was going to happen to her.

She pulled her curtains closed.

She wasn't going to give up yet, she thought as she let her towel drop to the floor and stepped into her undies and shorts. She would give this some time. She wouldn't wait for ever, but she was sure he felt something for her. And there was still time. She'd only been here a week. Besides, whatever happened with Mitch she was still keen for the Outback experience. It would look good on her résumé. Perhaps they both needed time to get used to the change. Although not much seemed to have changed for Mitch. He continued doing what she suspected he always did. Ran the station. He didn't spend a lot of time with the children. It was hard, she guessed, when he never got to leave work behind. It was a twenty-four-hours-a-day commitment.

She pulled a shirt from a hanger and slipped it over her head and opened her curtains again once she was decent. From her window she could see Mitch's figure as he stepped out onto the veranda. His tall, erect posture she'd know anywhere, although who else would it be? He had a beer in his hand. She boiled the kettle and made herself a green tea and carried it across the dry and dusty garden and climbed the stairs.

Mitch stood up from the old armchair as she arrived, his manners as impeccable as ever. She took the armchair next to him. The chairs faced outwards, looking across the garden and down to the creek. Not that she could see the creek bed as the sun had well and truly set. She sat quietly, letting her eyes get accustomed to the dark. There was a sliver of moonlight but the veranda was in darkness; switching on the lights only attracted the insects.

She could hear frogs croaking and the occasional plop as they hopped across the wooden floor. She was used to seeing them pop up in unexpected places. High on the glass doors, lurking in the toilet bowls, sitting startled in the middle of the floor when she flicked the light on at night. But they were such a vibrant green and so cute that she forgave them when they frightened the life out of her.

'Can I get you a beer?' Mitch asked. His voice startled her out of her reverie.

'No, thanks, I'm fine with my tea,' she replied as she turned to look at him.

He was leaning back in the chair, his bottom at the front, his long legs stretched out across the wooden boards. He'd showered too and his thick, dark hair was still slightly damp. He was wearing clean jeans, a button-down shirt that was open at the throat and had the sleeves rolled up. His forearms were tanned, his fingernails clean. He smelt divine, and he took her breath away.

'So, what did you need to talk to me about?' he asked, getting straight down to business. Maybe they weren't going to have the comfortable conversation she'd become used to in their late-night phone calls. Did he find it easier to talk to her over the phone or was he uncomfortable with his decision to bring her to the station? She hoped he hadn't changed his mind about her being here.

'A couple of things. I'll start with Lila.' She did actually need to talk to him about Lila and she figured she might be able to soften him up before she launched into the issue that was really concerning her. 'I need to make an ap-

pointment for her to see the physio but that will
mean a trip into Cunnamulla. Shirley said that's
a five-hour drive, is that right?'

Mitch nodded. 'Thereabouts.'

'So I needed to check—what's the best thing
to do? Which day would work best? Do I need
to take the boys too and can we stay in town
for the night? I don't think I want to drive back
in the dark.' Rose thought she was managing
well with the basics but there were so many
other things about living in the Outback that
she didn't understand.

'You want to go to Cunnamulla?'

'Yes. The physio clinic is there next week.'

'That would make sense. Cunnamulla have
their camp draft next weekend, they'll be tying
their outpatient clinics in with that, capitalising
on the influx of people into town.'

'Camp draft? What is that?'

'You'd probably imagine it to be a bit like a
rodeo. But it's a bit of a festival, an agricultural
show and some riding competitions all rolled
into one. People come into town from all over
the Outback, it's a chance to socialise and shop
but most will compete. There's a fair bit of prize
money involved. A few of our guys will be com-
peting and my kids usually enter some of the
children's events. We could all go a couple of

days early, sort out Lila's appointments and then stay for the camp draft.'

'We?'

'Of course. You have to experience at least one camp draft. But you'll have to be prepared to sleep in a tent. We'll take the camper trailer but it won't be five-star luxury.'

'That's okay.' It wasn't like she was used to five-star luxury anyway and, besides, she'd go anywhere, do anything if it meant she got to spend time with Mitch.

'All right, that's sorted. What's the other thing?'

She took a deep breath. 'I'm wondering if you're having second thoughts about me being here. I feel like you've been avoiding me.'

'I'm not avoiding you, Rose, I'm just busy. There's always something that needs my attention, a problem that needs fixing, an order that needs filling or a staff member who needs a solution.'

It sounded to her like he'd prepared his answer in advance. Was he telling the truth or making excuses?

'When you offered me the job, was that all you were offering? A job? Because I felt there was more to it.' It was unlike Rose to demand answers but she needed to know. She needed to be brave. What was the worst that could happen? Mitch could tell her he'd made a mistake. 'If you've changed your mind, just tell me.'

Mitch shook his head. 'I want you here but I haven't figured out yet where you fit in. I didn't really consider the fact that you'd be an employee. I'm not sure what to do with you.'

Rose smiled. That was good news. 'I've got a few ideas.'

'I have too, but it's difficult out here.' He smiled, but it was only a half-smile, not quite reaching his eyes. There was something bothering him.

'Is it because of Cara?'

'No. At least, not in the way I assume you're thinking. It's been almost two years. I admit I haven't been celibate since she died, although I certainly haven't been hitting the singles scene, but it's all been conducted away from the station. I'm just not sure how to do this under everyone's noses.'

'Are you worried about what they will think? It's okay to be happy. You don't need their permission.'

'No, it's not that. I'm just not sure that I want them all knowing my business. Or yours.'

'I don't care. I want to explore this thing between us.' Rose knew she'd been given a second chance at life and she was prepared to go after what she wanted. 'I'm not going to leave you in the lurch if you tell me you've changed your mind but I'm going crazy wondering what is going on in your head. Whether or not you're even thinking about me.'

'Trust me, I'm thinking about you.'

'I need to know what you want to do. I need something to assure me that I haven't made a mistake in coming here.'

'I realise that, I get it, I just need a bit more time.'

Rose stood up. Maybe she had to take no for an answer.

But Mitch hadn't finished. He stood up too. 'I understand what you're saying but I know that once I start I won't be able to stop. You know how quickly things escalated last time. Until I figure out all the practicalities I don't think I can afford to start.'

'But I can,' Rose said. She put her tea cup on the arm of the chair and lifted herself up onto tiptoe, bringing her level with Mitch. She over-balanced—missing toes did not make it easy—and as she wobbled Mitch reached out for her. His hands were on her arms, steadying her. She wrapped her arms over his shoulders and kissed him on the lips. If he wasn't going to take the initiative, she would. If her prince charming wasn't going to come and get her, she would go to him.

He pulled her in tightly against him, holding her close as he deepened the kiss. She parted her lips, offering herself to him, and he accepted.

She felt his response, hard against her belly, as their kiss became more urgent. He still wanted her, she knew that now, and suddenly her world seemed a little better, the stars a little brighter, the moon a little larger. Maybe everything would be all right.

This was what she'd been waiting for. This was what she wanted.

But it was over almost before it began. Apparently Mitch had other ideas. She felt his hands release her before he put them back on her upper arms, forcing her back from him, breaking their contact and ending the kiss.

'Not yet,' he said as he let her go. 'I need some time and there's more you need to know. I have to head out on a muster. There are some cattle I need to collect and I'll be gone for a few days. I need you to hold the fort with the children but I promise I'll work this out.'

'Are you sure this isn't just another avoidance tactic?' Before she'd left Adelaide for the station Mitch had explained the governess's job and all it encompassed. It was far more than just a nine to three, normal school hours job. He needed help with the children on a far more constant basis. She was happy to help but not if he was making excuses.

'No, it's not. I admit it's not great timing but I have to sell off some more stock and unless we get rain soon I'll have to keep selling.'

'When are you going?'

'Tomorrow.' He reached out a hand and picked up some strands of her hair, letting them fall through his fingers. 'Can we talk about this again when I get back?'

Rose nodded. She didn't see that she had much choice. She'd signed a contract. She had a job to do and she would do it but she wished she had a personal contract as well. Maybe then she wouldn't feel quite so left out in the cold.

CHAPTER EIGHT

MITCH WAS OUT on the muster and the station seemed bigger and emptier without him. It was ridiculous to feel lonely when there were a dozen other people around but some of the gloss had worn off with his absence. Even though she hadn't spent much time with him she'd known he was there, just across the flower garden or in the sheds or the cattle yards. Now, although technically he was still on the station, he was not in sight. He was miles away and would be gone for days.

To keep busy and distract herself she planned a host of extra activities for the children. They had cooked, planted a vegetable garden, taken part in a School of the Air music lesson and each day the boys kicked the soccer ball while she helped Lila with her physiotherapy and exercises. Today she decided they'd all go to the stables after therapy. Mitch wasn't due back until tomorrow and she figured another riding lesson would help to fill in the time. She got the boys to bring Ruff into the house first. She wasn't prepared to risk another episode of Ruff versus Fudge so she shut the little dog into the wire enclosure the mechanic had made and gave him a bone to keep him occupied.

Jimmy had given Rose four lessons so far and while she couldn't imagine ever being a confident rider she was beginning to feel a little more comfortable on horseback. At Lila's insistence, she'd been riding Fudge; Jimmy had agreed it would be good for Fudge to be exercised and she was an extremely gentle, placid horse, provided Ruff wasn't within cooee, and perfect for a beginner.

'Lemme saddle the boys' horses and then I'm gonna show you how to saddle Fudge today, Rose,' Jimmy said as she arrived at the stables.

This was the longest sentence Rose had heard Jimmy utter and she was so surprised she couldn't think of a response. Jimmy worked solely with the horses and usually had Fudge saddled in the time it took him to first see, or hear, Rose and the children making their way to the stables.

'You should know a coupla things about it, in case you ever need to adjust anything or if I'm not here.'

Rose thought it was unlikely that she would

be riding if Jimmy wasn't around but she didn't know enough to argue. If Jimmy was making the suggestion she figured there must be a good reason. He wouldn't be doing it just to make conversation. Silence didn't seem to bother him; in fact, Rose imagined he rather liked it. The peace and tranquillity of working with the horses seemed to suit him.

'Sure.'

Jimmy handed her a blanket to put under the saddle. The bits and pieces were familiar to Rose but adjusting the saddle and bridle were more difficult than she'd imagined. Jimmy showed her how to tighten the saddle and then wait for Fudge to breathe out before tightening it some more. It was only as Rose watched Jimmy pull on the leather straps that she realised he was missing two fingers on his left hand. She couldn't believe she hadn't noticed before. Jimmy was never more than a foot away from her when she was riding but she realised now that he always held the reins with his right hand. She wondered what had happened. His hand looked a little disfigured; it didn't look as if it was a congenital deformity but rather the result of an accident.

'Let me do that,' she said, the words popping out of her mouth before she had time to think about what she was saying and how Jimmy might construe her words. She was worried that he might not get enough force behind his grip before she realised that he'd been saddling Fudge every time for her and she hadn't had a mishap.

'It's fine. Me hand works perfectly fine, thanks to the boss.'

'The boss?'

'Yep. He saved me hand and me life.'

'That sounds awfully dramatic. What happened?' Once again the words were out before she thought about it. She knew she would hate it if anyone asked about her foot and yet here she was subjecting Jimmy to the same curiosity she would detest. 'Sorry,' she apologised, 'you don't have to tell me.'

'It's not a secret,' Jimmy replied. 'Everyone knows. It was a careless accident. I'd gone to kill a steer for the cook for dinner and I had a gun across me lap. It was loaded and the ute hit a pothole and the gun went off. Shot meself in the hand.' Jimmy shrugged. 'Coulda been worse.'

'That sounds pretty bad,' Rose said, although Jimmy didn't seem too perturbed.

'Nah. The boss stopped the bleeding. If he hadn't been there I reckon I woulda bled to death. Somehow he managed to save two of me fingers and me thumb and that's a whole heap better than it coulda been.'

While she was riding, Rose had no room in her head to think about anything other than staying in her saddle but once her lesson was finished and she and Lila were grooming Fudge she thought about what Jimmy had said. How could he be so matter-of-fact about losing two fingers? How could she not have noticed before? And, more importantly, why had Mitch given up medicine?

She thought about this as she got the children cleaned and ready for dinner. She had a surprise organised for them. She took them to the staff kitchen to collect their meal. She'd organised with Shirley to bundle up their dinner so she could take it back to the main house. She'd decided it was time for a change.

She'd decided they needed some table manners. They ate with the staff in the staff kitchen every night. There were four large tables in the staff kitchen and people tended to sit anywhere they chose, which meant Mitch and his children very rarely sat together for dinner. Rose understood it was easier for Mitch to feed the children in the staff kitchen but she didn't believe it was good for them as a family unit. She thought they'd benefit from having a weekly family dinner, just Mitch and his children, in their own house but she wasn't sure yet how she was going to raise the subject. In the mean-time she would trial it herself but she intended to make a game of it.

'Tonight we're going to eat at home,' she told the children as they collected the dishes.

'Home?' Lila queried. 'In our house?'

'Why can't we eat with everyone else?' Jed asked as Rose nodded and handed him a container of mashed potato.

'We're going to use our proper table manners. Knives and forks and serviettes.'

'Why?'

'Because it's something we all should know and practise. Besides, what if the Queen comes for dinner?'

Lila giggled and Jed laughed. 'As if the Queen would come all the way out here.'

'You know, Jed,' Shirley interrupted, 'when I was a lot younger, about thirty years ago, the Prince of Wales came to visit a station where I worked.'

'That was in the olden days!' Jed exclaimed.

Lila was more enthralled. 'Do you think the Queen really would come?' she asked Rose, her eyes wide.

'Maybe. Shall we all dress up just in case?'

Back at the house Rose put the dinner in the oven to keep warm while they rummaged through the dress-up box.

'I want to be a princess,' Lila announced as she chose a princess dress.

'Let's get the swords and shields,' Jed told Charlie. 'We're going to be knights. We can protect the Princess.'

'That means I can be the Queen,' Rose said as she found a shiny plastic tiara and popped it on her head.

The children set the table while she dished up the dinner and they were halfway through their meal when Mitch walked through the door.

Lila jumped out of her chair and threw her arms around Mitch's waist. Rose was tempted to do the same. She was equally as pleased to see him.

'You're back early. I wasn't expecting you until tomorrow,' she said.

Even dusty and with a three-day growth he was gorgeous and her heart did a little flip in her chest, matching the somersault that her stomach was doing. She'd missed seeing his face.

'We made better time than I planned. The guys are still out with the cattle but they're not far away so I thought I'd pop home and see what I was missing. It looks like I'm missing a party.'

'We're having schnitzels,' Jed told him.

'And practising for when the Queen comes for dinner,' Lila added.

'The Queen? I wonder what she would say if we served her schnitzels.'

'Rose is the Queen tonight,' Lila said. 'She likes schnitzels.'

'Yes, I am the Queen of Austria,' Rose said in an extremely bad accent.

'Did you say Australia?' Mitch laughed.

'No, Austria.' She smiled. 'Schnitzels originated in Austria, but I don't think theirs were made with beef.'

'Dad, did you know it snows in Austria?' Lila asked. 'We've been learning about it. And there's a song about schnitzels.'

Rose stood up to fetch another plate from the cupboard. 'Are you going to join us for dinner?'

'Daddy, you can be the King,' Charlie said.

'I don't think I'm dressed properly, and I need a shower first,' he said. He was looking at her intently and Rose had a fleeting, ridiculous notion that he'd come back for her and was almost surprised to find the children there with her. Had he made a decision? He'd told her he would. Dared she hope he was going to choose her?

Rose let him go. They could hardly have that conversation now, not in front of the children.

By the time Mitch returned the children had finished eating and were getting restless. They weren't used to sitting at the table unless there was food in front of them.

Jed pushed his chair back and stood up.

'Not so fast, Jed. You need to ask to be excused from the table.'

He looked at her in bewilderment.

'You put your knife and fork together like this,' Rose said as she moved her cutlery. 'That shows that you've had enough to eat, and you say, "May I be excused?"'

Jed copied Rose's instructions without complaint and Rose excused the children one by one. 'You need to clean your teeth for me, okay?'

Mitch grabbed a beer from the fridge. 'Can I get you one, too?' he offered.

'That sounds good,' she said.

Mitch twisted the top off before handing it to her and sitting at the table. 'So, how did it go? Did you have any problems while I was away?'

'Not at all. Your kids are delightful…'

'But…? Do I hear a but?'

'Not really.' She smiled. 'Well, maybe a little one. They may benefit from a bit more routine and structure.'

'Are they really wild?'

'Not yet, but there are a few things that could use some tweaking. Things like table manners. There's not much emphasis on that when they eat with the staff but I think it's important.'

'Is that what tonight was all about?'

'Partly. I thought it might be nice once in a

while to let the kids get used to a meal where they have to use their knife and fork properly and their manners.'

'Once in a while?'

'Once a week would be good. Just you and the kids. It would do them, and you, good to have some family time.'

'I'll think about it,' he said as the children came back into the living area. Lila was carrying the book Rose had been reading to them as their bedtime story.

'Why don't we read on the couch tonight?' she said to the children. 'That way your dad can listen to the story too.'

'Do you know this story, Dad?' Lila asked as she showed Mitch the book cover.

'It's about a magic tree.'

'It has all these funny people living in it.'

'And a slippery dip on the inside that you slide down on special cushions.'

'And the tree is huge and reaches right up into the clouds and magic lands come in the clouds to visit the tree.'

The children talked over the top of each other, eager to give Mitch their summary of the story so far.

'Okay, I think your dad has got the idea. Come and sit down quietly.'

Rose smiled at Mitch as she gathered the children together and settled them on the couch. Her smile lit a fire inside him, warming him from the inside. He was glad to be home. He sat at the table and listened to her read. It was peaceful and he almost couldn't remember what it was like before Rose had come to live there. A sense of calm came over him, as if this was how things were supposed to be.

His kids lay on the couch, draped across Rose. Charlie's head was in her lap and she was stroking his hair as she read. Jed was stretched out on one side of Rose and Lila lay curled on the other. Rose had one arm around Lila and Mitch wasn't sure how she was managing to turn the pages. He wanted to lie on the couch with his head in her lap too. He'd been missing her, wondering what she was up to. That was why he'd come back early. He'd wanted to see her. Needed to see her.

Rose reached the end of the chapter and he watched as his children hugged her goodnight. He could tell they'd done this before; it looked easy and effortless. They were used to having her here too and already he could see the changes Rose's presence had brought about in them. Lila was talking more—he hadn't noticed how quiet she'd become until he'd started to hear her voice again—and she and Jed had been getting on better. There'd been fewer arguments between them, or maybe Rose had just been handling them without involving him. Whatever she was doing was working. The house seemed calmer, more peaceful and happier since she had joined them. He felt all those things too.

He'd made the right decision, bringing her here. Now they had time to explore things further. He had time to do the right thing by Rose.

'Off to bed now,' she told them. 'Your dad will come and say goodnight in a minute.' She reached up and removed the tiara from her head as the children disappeared. 'I'd better get going,' she said as she loosened her hair. It fell in soft waves over her shoulders and she scooped it up, gathering it all in one hand and twisted it, draping it over one shoulder. He loved watching her do that. He found it mesmerising.

She was wearing a white dress that made her look like an angel. The dress had thin straps and hung loosely, skimming her body. Just two little flicks would knock those straps from her shoulders and the dress would fall to the floor. He could picture her naked, her blonde hair falling forward, covering one shoulder, one breast, and leaving the other breast exposed.

He closed his eyes but the image just intensified. Rose had been sleeping in his bed while he'd been away so the kids wouldn't be in the house alone, and he could imagine her lying on his sheets, her green eyes wide, her legs spread, waiting for him. He was getting aroused, growing hard. He shifted uncomfortably in his seat, trying to readjust himself surreptitiously.

He couldn't stand up and see her out. Not now. He needed a minute to recover from his fantasies. He'd been trying to ignore her, trying to ignore the attraction, his desire, but it was becoming impossible to deny.

'Stay and finish your beer,' he said.

She shook her head. 'I really should go.'

'I could use the company.' He really wasn't ready for her to leave. He'd come back to see her and he didn't want to sit here alone.

'Are you okay?' she asked.

No. I'm thinking about you naked. I want to tear that dress off you and make love to you. Right here. Right now. I don't think I can stand to wait any longer.

He ran his hands through his hair as he thought about how to answer her. Should he tell her what he was thinking? What he'd been thinking about for the past few days? Or should he talk to her about what he *should* have been thinking about? About all the stresses of the station that he'd been unable to concentrate on because his mind had been filled with thoughts and images of her.

'I'm okay,' he said, 'although sometimes I feel

like I'm barely keeping my head above water. There's a lot going on.'

She sat beside him at the table. 'It is a lot busier than I'd imagined. I thought you'd have a lot more spare time out here. I imagined that because you didn't have to go to an office, didn't have to commute, it would give you more time.'

'It's pretty all-consuming. There's always something that needs to be done. If it's not the cattle, it's the horses, or the machinery or paperwork or maintenance or staffing issues. It's really too much for one person. Cara used to do the paperwork, organise the trucks, order supplies. I have to do all of that too now. The only break I get is when I leave the station.'

'So you'll have to make the most of next weekend, then.'

'Next weekend?'

'The camp draft. We're all going to Cunnamulla, remember?'

He'd forgotten all about the camp draft and he knew it wasn't because he was busy. It was because, whenever Rose was nearby, he found it difficult to think of anything except her. 'I will.'

'I know it's not really any of my business but do you have a plan for the future? Perhaps you should employ someone to do the books? You can't be thinking that you can continue like this indefinitely?'

'Like what?'

'Burning the candle at both ends. It's not good for you or the children.'

'What do you mean, the children?'

'They hardly spend any time with you. They've lost their mother and their father is a shadowy figure on the periphery of their lives. I'm really happy to spend time with them, they're gorgeous kids, but they need you.'

Mitch sighed. He was trying to do his best, for everyone, but it seemed that wasn't good enough. 'There just aren't enough hours in the day. It's my job to keep this place running.'

'I understand that but you also have a responsibility to your children.'

'I'm doing the best I can. I don't know what else I can do.'

'Your kids just need some love and attention. You don't have to do anything specific. Just try to be there for them a little bit more. Spend some more time with them. I remember when my father died, my mother didn't cope very well. She was on her own with three children. I was the youngest, I was eight, so the issues were different, but I needed my mother and she wasn't really emotionally able to manage. All I wanted, all I needed, was to know that my mother was there for me. But she wasn't. Ruby went off the rails. A lack of supervision was not what she needed, and if it wasn't for Scarlett I'm not sure how I would have got through it.'

'What happened with your father?'

'He had an aortic aneurysm that burst. Completely out of the blue. My whole life changed in an instant. I *know* how your kids are feeling. They need your attention. I was the apple of my father's eye. He loved my sisters but I was special to him. I was his only child and I was also the baby.'

'Scarlett and Ruby are your half-sisters, is that right?'

Rose nodded. 'Mum has had a chequered love life. She fell pregnant with Scarlett when she was seventeen. Scarlett has never met her father. Ruby's father was a liar and a cheat. My father was the first one to give her, and my sisters, any sort of stability and normality. He adopted Scarlett and Ruby and for a while we were a perfectly normal, happy family. I was spoilt but I didn't know it at the time. I just accepted things as being the way they were because I didn't know any different.

'But when he died things changed. His life insurance was enough to pay off the mortgage on the house but Mum had to go back to work. That left Ruby with no supervision and me with no attention. I just needed someone to tuck me into bed at night and read me a story. I know

how your kids feel. They just want your attention. They've lost their mother, they need you.'

Cara had been the one holding them all together but she was gone now. Rose was right, he
was all the kids had now, he knew that, but that
didn't mean he knew how to handle it. Sometimes it was easier just to pretend everything
was okay and hope that would make it so.

'I know you're mostly around,' Rose continued. 'It's not like you disappear for twelve hours
a day but you seem a little distant. You were different in the city. More present. I know you're
good at the fun stuff but they need more from
you. They need love and cuddles. Not just a kiss
on the forehead.'

'I know they need more but it doesn't come
naturally to me,' he admitted. 'And I find it especially hard with Lila because she looks so
much like Cara.'

'Do you ever talk about Cara with them?'

'No.' He shook his head. 'They were so
young. They barely remember her.'

'Jed does,' Rose said, surprising him. 'Lila
even more so. I think she would like to hear
about her mum. I know Lila was only six but
she remembers.'

'I don't know if I can do this.'

'Of course you can.' Rose reached out and
put her hand on his hand. Offering comfort. He

turned his hand over and held onto hers, running his thumb over her palm. She watched him stroke her skin. 'I'll help you,' she said. 'Just spend some quiet time with them. Start with family dinner, just the four of you.'

'Cara used to feed the kids here at the house when they were small before they really ate Shirley's cooking,' Mitch said. Remembering Cara wasn't as painful as he'd thought. The pain had eased, softened, and he was able to look back without an ache in his heart. Did that also mean he was able to look forward? 'But after she died it was easier to eat in the kitchen quarters with everyone else. It was easier for me not to have to think about cooking for ourselves.'

'I'm not judging you. I'm trying to offer a suggestion. Mum worked night shift for seven years so that she could be home for dinner and back again in the morning before we went to school. Scarlett was there overnight but Mum must have been run ragged trying to manage everything else. I know it's not easy but you do have help. Shirley will cook for you, and you can just bring the meals back to the house like I did tonight. You can talk about your day. The kids will chat if you give them a chance. But if they always eat with the staff and sit at different tables you'll never hear about their thoughts. You won't form that bond. They need that routine. Even if it's just once a week. And read to them. Tuck them in at the end of the day. Spend some quiet time with them. Give them a chance to talk about anything. Listen to them.'

'That's the sort of thing Cara was good at.'

'You can learn. Little steps. You're good with the rough and tumble but they need some gentle affection too. You can do this.' Rose thought it would be good for Mitch too. 'It will help you all to heal. You can move forward together as a family.'

Rose fiddled with her empty beer. She really should go. Mitch needed to think. But she couldn't make her legs move. They sat at the table, looking at each other but not speaking. She'd said everything she needed to say about his family. There was only one other question that needed answering now.

She waited. Waited to see if he was going to say anything. Wanting to know if he'd come to a decision about them. But he was quiet.

She was going to bed.

She pushed her chair back from the table. 'I'll see you tomorrow,' she said as she pulled her hand from under his. Hesitating, she waited to see if he would take it back.

He didn't.

She stood and he stood too.

They were inches apart. She needed to feel

him and stepped forward and wrapped her arms around him, hugging him tightly. She figured he needed some human contact just as much as his kids did and kissed him softly on the cheek. 'Goodnight,' she said before stepping back. She could still see into his eyes, which were dark and unreadable. What was he thinking? He still wasn't speaking but she could feel the pull in the air, an invisible thread, holding them together.

He reached for her hand and pulled her back to him. With his other hand he tipped her chin up and bent his head and kissed her properly.

No questions. No answers.

The kiss was the question.

His lips were warm and soft but insistent.

Her response was the answer.

She opened her mouth under his pressure. Willingly acquiescing.

His hand was on the base of her spine. The pressure was firm, holding her to him. She could feel his body heat through the thin cotton of her dress. She wanted desperately to feel his fingers on her skin but instead she felt him pulling away.

'What's the matter? Have you not made a decision?' She'd promised herself she wouldn't beg or hassle him for an answer but she had to know. She had to know why he'd stopped and what he was planning on doing next.

'It's complicated.'

'Explain it to me. I think you owe me that.'

'You're my employee.'

'You pay me to take care of your children. What I decide to do in my spare time is not on the clock. It's not your responsibility.'

'But ethically?'

'How many times have you heard of the husband and the nanny having an affair? We're both single. We're not doing anything wrong. There's no law against it. Unless it's because of Cara? Are you not ready for this?'

'That's not the problem. I'm ready. When I'm not with you you're all I think about.' He ran his fingers down her arm, sending sparks from her chest to her groin. 'When I am with you I can't think of anything else but this. But my children are asleep across the hall.'

Rose smiled. She could solve that problem. 'I have a perfectly good bed a few feet away and there are no children in my house.' She could still see him hesitating. 'I've spent the past three nights here. If Charlie wakes up all he wants is a drink. Put some water next to his bed.' She doubted very much that any of the children would wake up. 'But it's your decision. You know where to find me.'

She kissed him again just to prove her point

and pressed against him, feeling his erection hard against her stomach.

She wondered what he would decide to do but it was up to him now. He had to come to her willingly, she needed to know he'd thought about things.

She let him go and walked away.

Mitch watched her go. He counted the steps as she crossed the flower bed and climbed up to her veranda. Fifteen. She was less than twenty metres away but she might as well be a thousand for all the comfort it brought him.

He went to kiss his children, who were all sleeping soundly, and then climbed into his bed. His head hit the pillow and he was assailed by Rose's scent. His linen smelt of her. If he hadn't come back early he knew she would have changed the sheets. He was glad she hadn't. Her scent was comforting.

He didn't want to be alone in his bed; he wanted her with him. He'd come back to see her, to have her. He'd opened the gate. He'd had a taste of her and, just as he'd anticipated, he wasn't going to be able to shut the gate now. He was finding her irresistible.

It scared him. So many people already relied on him, could he handle another?

He tossed and turned and knew sleep wasn't going to come easily.

Lying in his bed, he stared at the ceiling.

He didn't want to lie here alone. He wanted Rose.

He got out of bed and pulled on a pair of shorts.

He walked through the dark and silent house to the laundry, where he opened a cupboard. He pulled out a box and lifted the lid. The box contained all the things he'd packed away after he'd lost Cara and his daughter. Sheet sets for the cot, baby clothes, blankets and toys. At the time he couldn't bear to look at all those things. Each one was a reminder of what he'd lost but he hadn't been able to bring himself to give them away either.

But it had been months since he'd looked in this cupboard and now he couldn't say why he'd held onto all of this. Cara's clothes were gone. He'd kept her jewellery and her wedding dress and a few other things to pass on to the children, to Lila in particular, but he'd been able to give away the rest of his wife's things. But not these baby things.

He retrieved what he'd been looking for and shoved the rest of the things back into the box and closed the cupboard doors. He would sort this out soon. His life had changed. It had moved on. It had moved forward.

He picked up the baby monitor and the remote. He plugged the monitor into the hallway outside the children's rooms and put fresh batteries into the remote. He switched it on and then he took those first few steps.

He made his way across his veranda and over the dry and dusty flower bed and climbed the steps to Rose's house.

Moving forward.

CHAPTER NINE

A SOFT KNOCK on her door startled Rose.

She went to answer it, knowing it could only be Mitch, but that didn't lessen the surprise.

She hadn't really expected him to come over. She'd resigned herself to the fact that his resolve was stronger than his desire.

The hallway light illuminated his face but his eyes were dark, intense, and she knew he'd come for one thing and one thing only.

Her.

He lifted his hand. He was holding a baby monitor. Scarlett had the same one for Holly. Rose saw the green light shining; the unit was switched on.

She smiled and took his hand and pulled him inside before either of them could change their minds. Her heart was pounding and with a shaky hand she took the monitor from him and put it on the table in the hall.

Mitch gathered her in his arms and kissed her.

His fingers were at the back of her neck, under her hair, and they felt like heaven as his touch sent tingles shooting down her spine.

Her bedroom was to their right. There was no need to go any further into the house but now it was she who hesitated.

'Have I read this wrong?' Mitch asked as she stepped back. 'Have you changed your mind?'

'No. But there's a complication.'

'What is it? I seem to have become quite good at problem solving tonight.'

She'd spent the past few days wondering what he'd decide, hoping he'd choose her, but she still hadn't figured out what to do about the thing that scared her most. Her foot.

He smiled at her as he waited for her answer and Rose knew she'd have to figure something out. She wasn't going to pass up this opportunity again.

There was no way around it. She'd have to tell him.

She took a deep breath and gathered her courage. 'I have ugly feet.'

Mitch's smile widened and she could tell he was trying not to laugh.

'It's not funny.' She pouted.

'*That's* the complication? Whoever said feet had to be beautiful? They just have to get you from A to B.'

'Well, mine don't do that too well either.'

Mitch frowned. 'What are you talking about?'

She had to tell him. This was never going to work otherwise.

'Remember how you commented on my terrible balance?'

'Yes.'

'There's a reason for that. Something I haven't told you.' Rose took another deep breath—inhale for four, exhale for eight. 'After I contracted meningococcal I had to have three toes amputated on my right foot. My foot is ugly.'

'Is that all?' Before she knew what was happening he had gathered her back into his arms. He held her close, held her tight, and she felt safe. She rested her head on his chest. 'Did you think I wouldn't find out?' he asked.

'I know it makes me sound vain and shallow but my foot is really ugly.'

'So what were you planning on doing? Making love under the covers with the lights out?' She could hear the smile in his voice. She knew he was teasing her but she also knew her declaration hadn't fazed him in the slightest.

'That would be one solution,' she replied. He might think he wasn't bothered by her foot but he hadn't seen it yet.

'Did you really think I would care? I was a

doctor. I've seen plenty of things that are worse than a few missing toes and I know plenty of people who are missing bits. It doesn't change how I feel about them, it doesn't change how I treat them. It's a couple of toes.'

'I hate the way they look.'

Mitch stepped back and looked directly into her eyes. 'I'm not attracted to you because I thought you might have sexy feet. I'm attracted to you because you look like a gorgeous, golden angel. You are kind and gentle and you remind me of the good things in life. You make me smile and laugh and make me feel like I could be happy again. You are beautiful, and missing a couple of toes doesn't change any of those things about you, but if it would make you feel better why don't you get into bed, dim the lights and when you're comfortable, call for me?' He kissed her lightly on the lips. 'I'm not going anywhere. I'll wait right here.'

She had to trust him.

She nodded and did as he asked.

A short time later Mitch stepped into her room. He had removed his shirt in the passage and he dropped his shorts as he came through the doorway. He was naked and glorious and she forgot all about her foot. There was no room in her head for anything but the sight of Mitch, naked and ready and eager for her. She lifted the edge of the sheet and he joined her under the covers. His hands reached for her, pulling her to him, and under the light of the moon and to the background chorus of green tree frogs they made love in her bed and it was perfect.

He was gentle, understanding and considerate. He was all the things she'd hoped for and he made her feel whole again.

He was perfect.

She fell asleep with a smile on her lips and his voice in her ear. 'You are beautiful, Rose. Every inch of you.'

Rose spent the next week in a state of blissful delirium. Mitch was generous, attentive and thoughtful, not to mention gorgeous, and every evening he was hers, solely and totally and completely, for an hour or two.

They would share a drink on the veranda before he joined her in her bed before returning to his own.

She longed to be able to spend a whole night in his arms but she wasn't sure if that would ever happen and she was determined to make the most of the time she did get to spend with him.

If anyone noticed a change in their behaviour, nothing was said. They were all too busy getting ready for the camp draft. There was high excitement around the station as the preparations were made and that was enough to have everyone focussed on that and pay no heed to Rose and Mitch's activities.

Darren and Jimmy had taken the horse truck and gone on ahead to Cunnamulla. Mitch and Rose were taking the camper trailer and most of the staff were heading to the Outback town too. They'd earned some days off after the muster. Shirley was also going, taking advantage of having most staff off the station to have a break.

Mitch got their campsite organised before they took Lila to her X-ray and physiotherapy appointments.

'Lila is doing really well,' the physiotherapist told them. 'Her X-rays show good alignment and good bony union. She can start to take some more weight through her legs and we'll eventually be able to get rid of those crutches, but not just yet. It would be great to introduce hydrotherapy into her exercise routine now if we can organise it.'

'Hydrotherapy?' Mitch queried.

The physio nodded. 'Water-based exercises. Lila could do strengthening and mobility exercises in the water. The pool is warm and the water supports her weight. She can practise walking as well. We see some really good results but it all depends on whether it's something she can do at home. I can include Lila in our pool session tomorrow so you can see what exercises she would do. Do you have a pool?'

'No,' Mitch replied. 'But I might be able to figure something out.' Rose could see the wheels turning in his mind. 'How warm does the water need to be?'

'Thirty-four degrees is optimal.'

'I think we can manage to work something out.'

'So who wants to get in the pool with Lila?' the physio asked.

Rose blanched. 'I didn't bring my bathers.'

'You can wear shorts and a T-shirt if you have them.'

Mitch looked across at Rose. She'd gone as white as a ghost. He knew what the problem was. She wouldn't want to get into a public pool. She wouldn't want to go barefoot. He would sort the problem out but they didn't need to have this discussion in front of the physio. 'Tell us a time and we'll be there.'

He waited until they had some breathing space before raising the subject again. They were back at the showground, leaning on the fence, watching the first camp drafting event and waiting for Jimmy, who was the next competitor, to ride. 'It would make sense for us both to do the exercises with Lila, more sense for you

than me as I imagine you'll be the one super-
vising her back home,' he said.

'I don't have my bathers and I don't have my
aqua shoes. I can't get into a public pool.'

She looked terrified but he thought it was important for her to do this. She needed to take this
step. They both had healing to do and he knew
she needed to accept her disability and come to
terms with it. 'We'll do it together.'

'But what about the boys? Someone needs
to supervise them,' she said, making excuses.

'We brought half the station with us. Someone will help. I'm sure Shirley will be happy to
keep an eye on them.'

Rose shook her head. 'I don't want to get in
the pool. Please, don't make me.' Her voice was
shaking too.

'We'll go shopping. The hardware store will
have something you can wear on your feet. They
have a big boating and camping section.'

'Are you sure?'

'Positive. I'll be right there with you.' It wasn't
Lila who needed his support, it was Rose, and
he was happy to give it. 'I promise, you won't
have to get in the pool without shoes but I do
need you to know what Lila needs to do,' he
said just as Jimmy entered the arena.

A big cheer went up from the Emu Downs
crew and Jimmy was grinning from ear to ear as

he rode on the back of a beautiful, dark brown stallion. They watched as he attempted to complete the circuit around the barrels in the fastest possible time. He rode well and another cheer erupted as he finished to take the top spot in the competition so far.

'Can I ask you a question?' Mitch asked as Jimmy removed his hat and saluted the crowd.

Rose nodded.

'You know Jimmy had an accident on the station a few years ago and lost a couple of fingers, don't you?'

'Yes. He told me you saved the rest of his hand. That if you hadn't been there he would have died. Bled to death. He told me you saved his life.'

'Quite possibly.' Mitch brushed her comments aside. 'But that's not the point I'm trying to make. When did you notice that Jimmy was missing his fingers?'

'When he was saddling the horse for me.'

'So you didn't notice when you first met him?'

'No. I didn't notice the first few times he saddled the horses either, I only noticed because he was teaching me how to saddle Fudge so I was paying close attention. When he was tightening the straps, that's when I noticed.'

'And when you watch him ride, what do you see?'

'Someone who is very good at what he does and clearly loves it.'

'So watching him you wouldn't guess or even notice that he's missing two fingers of his left hand, even though you know that's the case?'

Rose shook her head.

'I know your foot is a big deal to you,' Mitch said. 'I understand that, but I guess what I'm trying to say is that most people won't even notice. People are generally not that observant. We're all too caught up in our own world, our own problems. A few missing toes doesn't change the person you are. It doesn't make you any more or any less than you were before and I hate to think of you letting it stop you from doing things. You are more than the sum of your parts. I'm not expecting you to do anything that makes you uncomfortable but I think you are giving this much more significance than it deserves. Don't think of yourself in terms of what's missing, think of yourself in terms of what you do have. You are beautiful and kind and you bring joy into my life and my kids' lives. Think about that.'

'Really?'

'Really,' he repeated as he wrapped an arm around her shoulders. 'Shall we go and get you some shoes?'

* * *

Rose was in Mitch's arms as he guided her around the dance floor. The tempo of the music had changed as the evening wore on and Rose was happy to be in his embrace. No one would think it was strange. There were plenty of other couples dancing the same way, some more closely than others.

They'd had an action-packed day. The boys had competed in their camp drafting events, they'd gone to the pool for Lila's hydrotherapy session and enjoyed the various sideshow rides and games before dinner. Rose knew she should be thinking about getting the kids into bed but she couldn't bring herself to leave Mitch. Maybe just one more dance. The kids were happy playing with their friends.

Mitch's long fingers were splayed across her back. She could feel the heat of them through her cotton shirt. She felt clumsy dancing in her riding boots, she found it difficult to change direction quickly, but dancing with Mitch was much easier than dancing alone. Mitch supported her. Physically and emotionally. In his arms she could forget about her feet. Her missing toes didn't bother him and she was beginning to think about not letting them bother her. In his arms she felt whole. In his arms she felt beautiful.

She closed her eyes but resisted the temptation to rest her head on his chest. She didn't want to encourage questions from the Emu Downs crew.

Rose stumbled as an overweight man bumped against her. Mitch arms tightened around her, holding her firmly and stopping her from falling.

'Are you okay?' Mitch asked.

As Rose nodded she noticed the man lurch and bump into a second dancer. Mitch reached out a hand to steady the man.

'Careful, mate,' he cautioned. 'Perhaps you should sit down, get a glass of water and stay off the booze.'

'He hasn't been drinking.' Rose noticed an elderly woman step up beside the man. She assumed she was the man's wife.

'At all?' Mitch queried with a frown.

The woman shook her head. 'Not a drop.' She looked worried.

Mitch looked concerned now too but Rose wasn't sure why. The man wasn't drunk, perhaps he'd just missed his step on the dance floor. But before Rose was able to ask Mitch what was bothering him the man clutched his stomach and collapsed at their feet.

Mitch dropped to his knees beside the elderly gentleman.

He had smelt alcohol on the man's breath. A sweet, slightly fruity odour that made him assume that the man had sneaked in a few drinks without his wife noticing.

The man's eyes rolled back in his head and Mitch shook him gently as his fingers probed the man's neck, searching automatically for the carotid pulse.

It was present, rapid but present.

He looked up at the man's wife, who looked ready to burst into tears.

'Are you positive he hasn't been drinking?' Mitch asked. He tried to keep his tone neutral, tried not to sound as though he was accusing her of lying. 'Could he have had a few without you noticing?'

The woman shook her head. 'We've been together all night. Stan hasn't been feeling a hundred per cent so I know he wouldn't have been drinking.'

'Stan, can you hear me?' Mitch used the man's name, hoping for a response while not actually expecting one. He had an accelerated heart rate, he smelt of alcohol and he was unresponsive.

If it looks like a rat… But Mitch knew that wasn't always the case. There were plenty of other conditions that mimicked drunkenness and this overweight, elderly man was certainly a candidate for several of the other options. Mitch needed support and Stan needed an ambulance.

He needed assessment and treatment. He needed to get to the hospital.

As Mitch thought about his options he heard Rose's voice.

'He's a doctor,' she said.

He wanted to protest. He was still licensed to practise but he chose not to. He didn't want to be in this situation. He didn't want to be the one everyone was relying on. What if he got things wrong?

He just wanted someone else to come and take over.

'Call the ambulance,' he instructed no one in particular.

The response he got was not the one he wanted. 'They're busy with a suspected heart attack on the other side of the showgrounds.'

He felt, rather than saw, Rose kneel beside him. 'What can I do?' she asked, assuming he had the situation under control. 'What do you need?'

'I need a medical kit and the local doctor.'

Rose stood up as Stan's wife leant over. 'What's wrong with him?' she wanted to know, but he ignored her question. He didn't know the answer, although he could hazard a guess, but guesses weren't helpful at a time like this. Instead, he answered her question with one of his own.

'Does he have any pre-existing health problems?' Mitch could see that Stan was overweight, flushed in the face. 'Any history of heart disease, diabetes, high blood pressure, allergies, liver damage?' The list was by no means exhaustive but it would give his wife an idea of what Mitch needed to know. He searched the man's wrists, checking for a medical ID bracelet.

Stan's wife shook her head.

'He's not diabetic?' Mitch queried. He would have put money on Stan being diabetic. This collapse looked suspiciously like a hyperglycaemic attack, which could lead to a coma if untreated.

'He's had some tests done but we haven't got the results back yet,' Stan's wife explained.

'We've called for the doctor.' Rose was back. 'What do you think is wrong with him?'

'It might be a diabetic coma. High blood sugar.'

'I can help you. Just tell me what you need me to do.'

He looked at Rose and she nodded her head. He knew she was telling him he could do this. That she trusted him. But did he trust himself?

Did he have a choice?

He knew he didn't.

'I need a testing kit,' he said as he raised his

voice. 'Is anyone here diabetic? Does anyone have a kit I can use?'

A small black case was handed to him. He pulled out the kit, pricked Stan's finger and squeezed the blood onto the testing strip. He slotted it into the machine and waited for the reading: BSL thirty-five mmol/litre.

He looked up and held out the testing kit, waiting for the owner to claim it. A teenage boy stepped forward and took the kit.

'Can you run to find the ambos?' Mitch asked him. 'Tell them I need an infusion set—IV fluids, a kit and electrolytes—tell them it's for a diabetic.'

Mitch saw the boy glance at the screen before he slid the kit into the bag. 'Do I tell them it's a hyperglycaemic attack?'

'Yep, thanks, mate.'

He didn't bother stressing that he needed the ambulance officers too, they would know they were required as soon as they were able to come. Mitch wondered where the local doctor was. Perhaps he'd already been called to help the ambos.

'Is he going to be all right?' Stan's wife asked as they waited.

Mitch hoped so. 'If we can get the fluids into him.'

The kid was fast. He was back with the infusion kit and handed Mitch another bag containing electrolytes, a syringe pack and a vial of insulin.

Mitch inserted the needle before replacing it with the catheter. It was a difficult process due to Stan's dehydration but Mitch was also worried that his hands would shake and disclose his nervousness but somehow he managed to attach the catheter and run the drip. He added potassium and sodium to the saline solution before giving Stan a shot of insulin.

He'd just finished when the local doctor arrived. He pulled up in a hearse and Stan's wife turned a shade of pale green and Mitch thought she might be about to faint.

The doctor pulled a spinal board from the back of the hearse and carried it across to Mitch. 'Sorry, the hearse is our only option for transporting a prostrate patient as the ambulance is still busy.'

Mitch nodded as he brought the local doctor up to speed. 'I've done all I can here,' Mitch concluded. 'We need to get him to the hospital.'

He helped to roll Stan onto the stretcher before lifting him into the hearse and telling his wife to hop in the front.

She still looked worried. 'Is he going to be all right?' she repeated.

'He'll come around once those fluids start

working and we get his blood sugar level back to normal,' he told her as he bundled her into the front of the hearse. The hospital staff could tell her more. That was their job. He was just a cattle rancher now.

CHAPTER TEN

ROSE HANDED MITCH a cup of coffee and sank into the camping chair by his side. The kids were finally in their sleeping bags, a lot later than planned due to the drama of the evening, but at least now they had five minutes to themselves.

She could hear music from the showgrounds, drifting on the slight breeze. The band had started up again. She found it hard to believe that the party was still going. She was exhausted. The adrenalin of the evening was wearing off and she could feel fatigue setting in but she knew she wouldn't be able to switch off and go to sleep. Not yet.

Mitch had been terrific tonight in a very confronting situation. Her own heart was still racing and she could only imagine how he was feeling.

'You were brilliant,' she told him as he took the cup.

'That's very generous of you. It wasn't a difficult diagnosis.'

'I didn't see anyone else with an idea,' she replied.

'It was nothing special. I'm just a country GP.'

It was the first time she'd heard him admit that he was still a doctor. Usually he protested the description, stating that he wasn't practising any more. Despite his lack of practice, he didn't seem to have lost his skills.

'I don't think anyone is *just* a country GP. You have such amazing skills, surely a part of you must miss it?' Rose had been amazed at how decisive Mitch had been. There'd been no hesitation on his part, he'd known exactly what to do. She couldn't understand why he had so much self-doubt. 'Is there no way you can live on the station and still practise?' She was certain that if he wanted it badly enough he could make it happen.

Mitch was silent for a long time. He sipped his coffee and she wondered whether he was going to answer her, or ignore her completely, when he finally spoke.

'Cara inherited the station when her brother died. It's belonged to her family for generations. She was the brains and when I was there I was the brawn, but I did continue to practise medicine. I used to go into Broken Hill once a week; I'd work three days in a row in the medical clinic and then drive home. But it all became too hard after she died. I couldn't afford to be away from the station for days at a time. I couldn't afford to be away from the kids. I had responsibilities—running the station for one thing, the kids for another.'

'You could have sold it. Moved to town and continued to practise medicine.'

He shook his head. 'It's the kids' inheritance. I couldn't make that decision.' It was also his connection to Cara. His wife and daughter were buried on Emu Downs. He couldn't abandon them. He had failed them in life, he wouldn't do the same now they were gone.

'Would you go back to it if you could? I could look after the children if you wanted to.'

'I appreciate your offer but the children are the least of my problems. Running the station is all-consuming in time and energy. I can't do both, not even with your help, and I don't want to. It's okay.'

But he knew he was telling a white lie. It wasn't okay, he did miss medicine but he knew he wouldn't practise again. He didn't trust himself.

And one good outcome tonight was not enough to change his mind.

He couldn't have it all and he had to be content with that.

* * *

Rose wished she could work out how to convince Mitch that he should use his medical training. She supposed his argument of being time poor was a valid one but it seemed such a waste of an obvious talent. She was almost positive that he'd taken pride in his diagnosis and treatment of Stan under difficult circumstances. When they'd checked on him the next day they'd found him in high spirits, having made a good recovery.

But every time she tried to raise the topic with Mitch he changed the subject.

She was getting nowhere and on the second Sunday in May she decided to give the argument a rest. It looked like one she wasn't going to win.

It was Mothers' Day and, although they hadn't discussed it, Rose imagined that Mitch would be finding the day tough to cope with. He was short-tempered with the children on a couple of occasions in the morning, which was unlike him, and Rose decided the best course of action would be to keep the children occupied and out of his way. She didn't want to add to his stress level if she could avoid it.

She took the kids to the kitchen and together they baked a cake for Shirley before Rose took them all to the concrete water tank that Mitch had filled with warm artesian water and converted into a hydrotherapy pool for Lila. She and the children enjoyed their day and she hoped she'd successfully given Mitch some breathing space.

Lila loved the freedom of movement that being in the warm water gave her and Rose could see obvious improvement in her strength and mobility. Each little step forward that Lila made also helped to bolster her confidence and the one-on-one time they spent together was encouraging Lila to confide in Rose. And just as Rose could see the changes in Lila she could feel them in herself too. Station life suited her, she'd decided. She was blossoming too. She was feeling stronger and fitter from the combination of hydrotherapy and horse-riding and her night-time activities with Mitch didn't hurt either. Now she just had to figure out how to get him to ask her to stay.

'Are you okay?' she asked him later that evening when they were alone together on his veranda.

'Mmm…' His reply was very noncommittal.

'Today must be hard for you,' she persisted. 'Are you missing Cara?'

Mitch didn't answer immediately before saying, 'It's not about me. I'm just feeling sad for my children who are going to grow up without knowing their mother. It seems worse on Mothers' Day.'

'You could talk to them about her. You can keep her memory alive for them.'

'I wouldn't know what to tell them.'

'Tell them about when you first met. When you fell in love. Tell me.'

'You want me to talk about Cara?'

Rose wasn't sure that she wanted to hear that story but she knew it was important. If she wanted the chance of a future with Mitch she needed to understand his past and he needed to share his feelings with her. She nodded. She wouldn't know where she stood until she understood his relationship with Cara and what it had been like. After all, Cara was the mother of his children. Rose didn't intend to replace her; she respected the fact that the children should have some knowledge of their mother, even if they didn't have the memories.

'We met at university in Brisbane. I was living in the same university boarding house as her brother, Peter. He was doing agricultural science and I was at med school. We were two years older than Cara but she followed in Pete's footsteps. She came to the city to study agricultural science too but she had dreams of being an artist. I'd visited the station with Pete so I'd met Cara before she came to the city but we didn't start dating until she moved to town. She asked me out—I wasn't sure that it was a good idea to date a friend's sister but she had other plans,' he told her.

'When she finished her degree she stayed in the city to be with me and went to art school. We moved to Broken Hill so I could do my GP training. It was close to the station, her parents and Pete, who was running the station by then, plus it's a big arts community.

'We got married around the same time but when Pete was killed in a light plane crash nine years ago we moved here. I continued to work in Broken Hill, travelling down to work three consecutive days and then travelling back while Cara ran the station. Then her mum was diagnosed with cancer and her parents moved to the city to be closer to treatment.

'Now I'm the only one left. The station is mine. I never wanted to inherit it, it wasn't my plan. Pete should still be here but now I can't let it go. It's the children's legacy, I'm just the custodian. It's a link to their family history, a family that's gone now. It's all that's left for them.'

Rose wondered how different Mitch's life would be if Cara hadn't asked him out all those years ago. He wouldn't have experienced the heartache he'd suffered but neither would he have his children. Which meant she would probably never have met him. She didn't want him to hurt any more, he'd suffered enough. He'd lost one of his best friends, his wife and given up his career. She wished she knew how to help. 'After she died, that's when you quit medicine?'

Mitch nodded. 'I told you it was because I had too much on my plate, that I couldn't manage it all, but that's not the whole truth. I could have chosen medicine over the station. I do feel like I'm the custodian, keeping the station for the children, but there would have been no one to stop me if I'd decided to sell up, move to town and continue to practise medicine. The only person stopping me was me. I gave up medicine not because I couldn't practise but because I didn't want to continue. I hadn't been able to save Cara and I lost faith in my ability as a doctor. No one wants a doctor who can't trust his own judgement. Who can't trust himself.'

But she'd seen Mitch in action. She knew he still had the instincts of a good doctor. How could he give that up? What had happened that had made him throw that all away? She needed to know. She needed to understand.

'What happened?'

'Cara was pregnant when she died.'

'Pregnant?' Rose hadn't known that. He'd lost his wife *and* a child?

'She was twenty-one weeks. I lost them both

on the same day. I'd been in Broken Hill, working at the medical clinic for my usual three days. When I got home Shirley was looking after the other children. She told me that Cara had complained of a headache, nothing serious, but she'd gone to lie down. It turned out she'd had a headache for a few days but neither she nor Shirley had given it much thought.

'Cara had an appointment in town for an antenatal check coming up but she hadn't thought a headache warranted a need to go sooner or to call for the flying doctor or even to let me know. It was just a headache and Cara didn't think it was related to the pregnancy. She'd had three other pregnancies without any issues and delivered healthy babies. She was only thirty-four and not considered high risk as her other pregnancies had all been straightforward. She didn't think there was anything seriously the matter.

'But she was wrong.

'She had gestational diabetes. Her blood pressure was skyrocketing, which was causing the headache, but it was more serious than that. She'd developed pre-eclampsia that was undetected and progressed into eclampsia and by the time I got back it was too late.

'When I went to check on her she was convulsing. Then she had a stroke. By the time the flying doctor got here she was unconscious. She was still alive but they were too late. She died on the way to the hospital.

'If I'd been here, on the station, instead of in Broken Hill, I could have saved her.'

'How? You said she had a stroke.'

'I could have diagnosed the pre-eclampsia. I would have recognised the signs. The high blood pressure, the swelling of her hands, feet and face. Once detected it can be managed. Not cured but managed.'

'What could you have possibly done?'

'I could have given her magnesium sulphate to prevent more seizures but I wasn't here. I was too late.'

'You weren't to know.'

'I know but if we didn't live out here she might have been saved. This place, it's beautiful but it's so harsh. There's no margin for error. Help is so far away. If I'd been here or if we'd lived in town she would have survived.'

'And the baby?'

Mitch shook his head. 'A little girl. I admit, even if I'd been home I might not have been able to save her. The only cure for pre-eclampsia is to deliver the baby. More than likely she would have been too premature to survive. But you never know. I lost them both that day. It was the worst day of my life and something I hope I never have to go through again.'

Mitch was restless now. He stood and paced the veranda. 'I need to go for a walk. Will you come with me? The kids will be all right.'

He reached for her and pulled her to her feet. He kept hold of her hand and they walked in silence up the hill behind the house and down the other side. There was an old stone building that she'd never noticed sitting in a stand of eucalypts. Not a building really, the roof had long since rotted and the walls were crumbling, and behind the building, among the gum trees, she could see a cluster of tombstones. How had she never noticed these before?

Mitch let go of her hand and squatted down in front of the two newest stones.

In the moonlight Rose could read the inscriptions.

One was engraved with Peter's name. The other with Cara's.

There were fresh frangipani flowers on the headstones and Rose knew Mitch had already been there once today.

She read the inscription.

Cara Louise, beloved wife and mother
10th October 1980—7th May 2015

May Louise, beloved daughter and sister
Gone with the angels
7th May 2015

The seventh of May was today's date. It was the two-year anniversary of their death.

'It's today?'

Her heart ached for Mitch. For everything he'd lost. She knew the pain of loss but nothing on this scale. To lose a wife and child at the same time, how did someone recover from that?

'You called her May.'

'She was born at twenty-one weeks so I had to register her birth,' Mitch said as he stood up. His voice was heavy in his throat. 'We hadn't chosen a name yet. I named her May after the month she was born but I didn't think about how it would make me struggle every year, every May, that came after. I didn't think about how it would continue to affect me. I didn't know.'

He sat down wearily on the crumbling stone wall of the old building.

Rose took his hand. To make matters worse, this year, the anniversary of their death coincided with Mothers' Day. She fought back tears. She hated to see him hurting but this wasn't about her feelings. She just wanted to take his pain away.

He was staring at their hands, at their entwined fingers. 'I haven't practised medicine since that day,' he said.

Rose had wondered what had really prompted Mitch to give up medicine. From what she had seen he had a natural affinity with people, an instinctive desire to help, and he hadn't lost his ability to make quick and accurate decisions. She'd wondered what had made him walk away from all that but she hadn't imagined the catalyst would have been the deaths of his wife and unborn daughter. That scale of tragedy was impossible for her to imagine. 'It wasn't your fault,' she told him.

'I'm still not sure about that. It makes it hard to forgive myself.'

'Mitch, I've seen you work. I know you would have done everything possible. There are some things you can't control in life. You taught me that. You don't need forgiveness if you're not to blame.'

She waited for him to look at her, to acknowledge her words. He had helped her to accept her past and shown her how to move forward with her life. She would give anything to be able to help him do the same. She hated to see him hurting but she wasn't sure what she could do to ease his pain.

She needed to get his mind off the past. Dwelling on those tragic events wasn't going to help anyone. She leant towards him, not sure if her overtures would be accepted or rejected, and kissed him.

He kissed her back before asking, 'What do you see in an old man like me?' as if he couldn't understand what she was doing there.

'So many things,' she said, 'but mostly you just take my breath away. You did from the moment I first saw you.'

She stood up, still holding his hand, and led him back to her house. She took him to her bed, there were no old memories for him there, and comforted him as she'd learnt how to.

She lay awake once they were spent, holding him in her arms and wondering about the future. Their future.

Mitch was a good man, a passionate, kind and considerate man. He was a good father and he'd been a loving husband and Rose knew she was in love with him.

He had given her a gift. He'd opened her up to a world where love was possible. She was able to see herself through his eyes now. She had grown and matured and she had accepted the new version of herself because he had made her believe. He had made her stronger.

In her fantasies about her future she'd always imagined that her prince charming would sweep her off her feet and take care of her but now she knew she could take care of herself and also of others. She wasn't going to be the damsel in distress, she was going to bring this family back to life. Spending time with them, loving them, had restored her soul and her self-confidence, and now she knew she was strong enough to restore him too. If he would let her.

She loved him but she didn't know if that was enough. She didn't know if that would make any difference because she didn't know if he would ever give himself permission to love again.

And she didn't know what that would mean for them. Or for her.

CHAPTER ELEVEN

ROSE ROLLED OVER and hit the snooze button on her alarm. Just five more minutes. That was all she needed.

She was exhausted. Last night she'd driven back from Broken Hill, returning from a three-day sports camp with the children. She'd done all the driving as well as being wholly responsible for them while they'd been away and she was worn out. Adrenalin had kept her going on the drive home. The thought of seeing Mitch had kept her buzzing. She couldn't wait to touch him, to make love to him, and she'd barely been able to wait until the children were in bed before dragging him home with her. But after he'd left her bed, after she'd come back down to earth and after the adrenalin had left her body, she'd begun to feel unwell.

Initially she'd thought she was just worn out and all she needed was a good sleep but then she'd developed a sore throat and a headache and had become nauseous and feverish. She'd taken some pain relief during the night but hadn't been able to keep it down. God, she hoped whatever she had she hadn't passed onto Mitch. They didn't both need to feel like crap.

Hopefully he'd escaped whatever lurgy she'd contracted.

She closed her eyes. A few more minutes in bed and then she might be ready to face the day.

Mitch was at the cattle yards talking to Darren when Jed came flying around the corner. He skidded to a stop in the red dust and grabbed Mitch's hand. 'Dad, Dad, come quick.'

The hairs on the back of Mitch's neck stood up and a shiver of fear ran down his spine as he recalled the last time Jed had run towards him uttering those same words.

'Lila wants you. Rose is sick. She can't get out of bed.'

Rose. Not Lila. But his reaction was the same.

His heart turned to stone in his chest and plummeted into his stomach, making his insides churn. He fought back rising nausea. This couldn't be happening. Not again.

'I'll be back,' he said to Darren before sprinting in the direction of Rose's house, leaving Jed in his wake.

Lila was waiting on the front veranda. She

looked worried and he had a brief, fleeting thought that an eight-year-old shouldn't look like that but he didn't have time to stop. He took the steps two at a time, flung open the screen door and burst into Rose's bedroom. Her room was dark but even so he could see that her cheeks were flushed and he could tell just by looking at her that she had a fever.

As he sat on the bed beside her his foot knocked against a bucket that was on the floor. She'd been vomiting. He put his hand to her forehead. Her temperature was raging; she was burning hot under his fingers.

She opened her eyes at his touch. Her eyes, which were normally the soft green of an emu egg, were dull and feverish.

'Hi.' Her lips were dry and parched and he could see the effort she went to just to speak.

He didn't take his eyes off her as he spoke to Lila, who was hovering anxiously at his shoulder. 'Lila, go to the bathroom and run a hand towel under cool water and bring it back to me,' he said. He needed to cool Rose down.

She was too sick to get out of bed and he knew that was not a good sign. If she'd been feeling just a little poorly she would've made an effort to get up. The fact that she hadn't, when she should be in the classroom with the children, spoke volumes.

He needed some light, he needed to see her clearly. 'I have to open the blinds,' he said as he stood up. He raised the blinds and saw her wince as light streamed into the room.

She was dehydrated. He could tell from looking at her lips and her tongue. He gently pinched the skin on her arm. The skin tented, not resuming its normal resting phase.

'Tell me what's wrong,' he begged. 'Tell me what hurts.'

'My head and my throat.' Her voice was hoarse.

'Have you taken anything?'

She nodded slowly. 'But I can't keep it down.'

She must have picked up an infection in Broken Hill. He could feel a sweat breaking out on his forehead and back. A cold, nervous sweat. His heart was racing, gripped by icy fingers of fear. He tried to bite it back but the heavy feeling of dread settled in his stomach.

This could not be happening again.

To him or to her.

She'd been fine last night, hadn't she?

He'd been so eager to see her, to get her into bed, had his eagerness clouded his judgement? Had he really lost all his clinical reasoning skills, all his powers of observation?

Could she have been this sick and he hadn't noticed? Was it simply a virus or something more sinister? He knew it was rare but not impossible to contract meningitis more than once. It was unlikely but he couldn't afford to ignore the possibility. He couldn't afford another mistake.

He sent the children outside and then pulled down the sheet that covered Rose. His heart was in his throat as he checked her skin for a rash. It all came back to him and he knew what to look for. He just hoped he was wrong.

He breathed out when he saw her skin was clear. He hadn't even realised he'd been holding his breath.

'Can you tuck your chin onto your chest?' he asked, relieved to see that she was able to do that without difficulty. His slid his fingers around to the back of her neck, pressing gently over the vertebrae and then moving forward over her glands. 'Is that sore?'

'Just on my throat.'

She had no rash and her neck movements were okay but he could feel a wave of panic threatening to engulf him just the same. What if he was missing something?

'I'm calling the flying doctor.'

He watched as she swallowed, it looked painful, and then he listened as she forced the words out. 'Don't be silly. I must have picked up a bug. I'll spend a day in bed and I'll be fine.'

She wasn't confused, that was another good sign, but she was exhibiting several other symptoms similar to meningitis. She had a headache, a high temperature and sensitivity to light. He knew they could also indicate all manner of other illnesses but he wasn't prepared to take that chance.

He shook his head. 'I'll start you on a course of antibiotics but I'm also calling the flying doctor.' A precautionary dose of antibiotics wouldn't do her any harm but he wasn't prepared to stop there.

'Don't you think you're overreacting a little?'

He knew he might be but he wasn't about to admit it. In his opinion it was better to be safe than sorry. He wasn't going to make the same mistake twice. Even though last time he'd acted as quickly as he could it still hadn't been enough. He wasn't going to risk waiting until it was too late.

'You're not well and you've been vomiting, which means there's a chance you haven't kept your anti-rejection medications down either.' He sounded angry but in reality he was scared. 'You need a drip and a blood test. You need to be in hospital. We're too isolated here.'

He wasn't going to argue with her. He was making a decision. It wasn't safe to keep her here.

He kissed her on the forehead before he stood up. 'I'll make the phone call and come back with the antibiotics.'

The flying doctor had a plane available to leave immediately. He'd decided as he placed the call that if they were going to have to wait he'd get his pilot to get the Emu Downs plane ready. He would take her himself if it meant getting her there sooner. He wasn't going to regret not making a decision earlier. Not again.

Waiting for the flying doctor still meant a round trip instead of one way but their plane was faster and they would have the necessary drugs and equipment and, more importantly, Mitch knew they'd be able to make objective decisions about Rose's treatment. Their assessment wouldn't be clouded by emotions, regret or past mistakes. He knew it was better for everyone if he let the flying doctor take over, but it was difficult, immensely difficult, to sit and wait. He hated waiting.

Mitch paced restlessly at the edge of the airstrip as the plane departed, airlifting Rose to Broken Hill. He thought if he stood still he might pass out. Doc Burton had been his usual calm, unflappable self when he'd arrived to take over Rose's care but that hadn't settled Mitch's nerves. He was a dreadful patient and an even worse observer when someone he loved was suffering.

He grabbed hold of the fence post and closed his eyes, forcing back tears, as the realisation hit him.

He loved her.

He breathed deeply as he thought about what that meant.

It meant his decision to call the flying doctor had been the right one. He loved her and he had to keep her safe.

'Mitch?' He heard Shirley's voice and felt her hand on his shoulder. 'I think you should go to Broken Hill, you won't relax until you've seen her again.'

Shirley had been on the station for years. She'd been there when he'd lost Cara. 'I'll look after the children,' she offered. 'Just go.'

Mitch didn't hesitate. He made the five-hour drive in a little over four hours but he barely remembered it. He parked in one of the doctors' bays in front of the hospital and didn't stop until he had to wash his hands before entering the intensive care unit.

'Joanna,' he greeted the doctor on the unit. She was a former colleague of his.

'Mitch! What are you doing here?'

'I'm looking for Rose Anderson; she was air-lifted from Emu Downs.'

'She's in here,' Joanna said, indicating an isolation bed.

Fear split Mitch's heart in two. Jo took one look at his expression and added hastily, 'It's just precautionary. She's had blood tests, I'm pretty sure it's not meningitis.'

'Pretty sure?' He could feel his hand shaking as he fought to keep his emotions in control. 'Are you going to do a lumbar puncture? You know she's had bacterial meningitis before?'

'Yes, I know. And she's had a kidney transplant, but there's nothing to suggest that she has meningitis again. If I see anything that makes me suspect otherwise, I'll order further tests. She's on a drip and IV antibiotics. We'll monitor her closely for the next few hours. You're welcome to sit with her but you have to trust me to do my job. Okay?'

Mitch nodded. He gloved and gowned and donned a face mask just in case and then sat by Rose's bed while she slept.

His guilt threatened to overwhelm him. He couldn't believe he'd put her at risk by being so isolated.

He made another decision while he sat beside her.

This time he was going to listen to his head instead of his heart.

He held her hand and put his head on her mattress. He dozed off but woke when he felt her stir.

She looked confused but her green eyes were brighter and a little bit of hope flared in his chest. 'Hi.'

'Where am I?'

'Broken Hill hospital.'

'What are you doing here?'

'I had to make sure you were okay. I had to see for myself. How are you feeling?'

'Better,' she said as he put his hand to her forehead.

Her temperature had come down, so had her blood pressure and heart rate. He knew from her observations that she should be feeling better but he was still worried. He needed to sort out what was going to happen next, before he changed his mind.

'I have good news. The doctors think it's most likely just a mild virus. A common cold you must have picked up at the sports camp.'

Rose smiled. 'I told you it was nothing.'

'It's not nothing. The station is no place for you. It might have been minor this time but what if next time it isn't? It's not safe for you to be stuck out in the middle of nowhere.'

'What do you mean, "It's not safe"?'

'This is exactly what I was afraid of. Of you getting sick and being so far from help.'

'You were also afraid of sleeping with an employee, of what people would think, but that hasn't stopped you. Hasn't stopped us.'

'I was worried about that, not afraid. It's completely different.' But none of those things actually came close to his biggest fear, *I was afraid of losing you.* But he couldn't bring himself to say that. He was afraid that giving that fear a voice would strengthen it somehow. 'I can't risk losing anyone else.'

He'd lost Cara because of the remoteness and he wasn't about to risk the same thing happening with Rose. He couldn't guarantee her safety in the Outback but he couldn't leave the station either. He had an obligation to his children, it was their inheritance.

He had resigned himself to being alone.

'I'm tough. I survived meningitis, I'll survive this. You said it's only a cold.'

Mitch was shaking his head. 'But what if next time it's something more serious? What then? Your immune system is already suppressed, which makes you more susceptible to illness. I can't keep you safe. You need to go home.'

'*What?* You're sending me away?'

'I've already lost my wife and daughter. This is a risk I'm not prepared to take.'

'You can't do that! I love you.'

Mitch was silent. He looked like he had the weight of the world on his shoulders. If only he would listen to her, if only she could make him understand—she could *share* his worries, she didn't need to contribute to them.

He was still shaking his head. 'I'm not what you need.'

'Maybe, maybe not. But you are what I *want*. You and your children. I love you all.'

'I'm doing this for your sake, Rose. It's not safe. I'll get Shirley to pack your things and send them down to you.'

'Don't you dare!' she said as tears spilled from her eyes. It felt like a little piece of her heart had been ripped off and lodged in her throat. She struggled to talk. 'You can send me away.' She knew he could, she couldn't stay on at the station if she wasn't invited or employed to. 'But please don't make me leave without saying goodbye to the children. I love your kids. I'm not going to abandon them. They've lost too many people already without the chance to say goodbye. You can't ask me to do that.' Her fate rested completely in his hands but surely he couldn't expect her to leave without saying goodbye?

* * *

Lila and Shirley were helping Rose pack her things. Mitch had agreed to let her return to the station but he hadn't given an inch on any of his other conditions.

Steve was flying her back to Broken Hill today and she would be on the bus bound for Adelaide this evening. She wasn't going to get her happily ever after.

She stood in the middle of the school room, trying to work out what to take with her. The walls were covered with the children's artwork and she'd love to take some home as a memory of her time here, but she didn't want to strip the walls. She didn't want to lay them bare. It would feel too much like her heart.

A map of the world was taped to one wall along with the lyrics for the song about schnitzels with noodles. Rose didn't want to think about all the days she'd spent with the children and all the things she was going to miss. She picked up her laptop and zipped it into its case as she fought back tears.

'Why are you leaving?' Lila asked for what felt like the hundredth time.

'I have to get well,' Rose replied, giving her the same answer she'd given every time.

'You're coming back, though, aren't you? When you're better?'

'I…' Rose didn't have the words for that answer. It was breaking her heart to leave and to know that this was goodbye. To know she wouldn't be back.

'We'll have to wait and see,' Shirley said, jumping in to fill the silence. 'It'll be a nice surprise if Rose comes back, won't it?'

Rose bent down to kiss the children one last time. She wrapped them tightly in her arms, taking a minute to remember the feeling of their little bodies pressed against her as they hugged her back. She'd said goodbye to everyone else, Jimmy, Darren, Shirley, and asked them not to come to the airstrip. She'd told them it would make her too upset but the reality was she just wanted one last moment alone with Mitch and the children.

She'd always wanted a family of her own but now she knew she didn't have to have children of her own. That was something she'd feared might not be possible after her transplant, although she'd been told it wasn't an issue. The only problem was being unable to breastfeed because of the immunosuppressant medication but she'd figured that would be a small price to pay. Now she didn't care about having babies of her own, everything she wanted was right here in front of her and about to be taken away and there was absolutely nothing she could do. She had begged and pleaded with Mitch to see reason but he'd remained steadfast, stubborn and resolute. He didn't want her and she had to get on with her life.

She couldn't stay.

He didn't love her. He certainly hadn't told her he did but she took a small slice of satisfaction as he hugged her tightly one last time and didn't hurry to let her go. She thought she could see pain in his eyes and she hoped it was hurting him to say goodbye, just like it was hurting her.

She knew he was afraid of letting himself love again, but that didn't make it any easier to walk away.

The sunlight reflected off the little plane as it took to the sky. It was another gorgeous autumn day—sunny, bright and cheerful. It was the complete antithesis of Mitch's feelings but he'd brought this upon himself. This was all his doing, he thought as he watched the plane fade into the distance, taking Rose with it.

'What the hell are you doing, letting her go?'

Mitch turned to see Shirley standing behind him. He hadn't heard her arrive at the airstrip.

She had her hands on her generous hips and she looked ready to box him around the ears.

'Are you crazy?' she added. 'Now what are you going to do?'

'Nothing.'

'Nothing!' She threw her hands in the air. 'I can't believe you. It's obvious you have feelings for each other. What's wrong with taking another chance at happiness?'

'I can't keep her safe. I can't risk losing her.'

'Looks to me like that's what just happened.'

'Leave it, Shirl.'

'Just tell me this,' she said, ignoring his pleas. 'How is letting her go any different? She's gone either way. She has a brain in her head. She can make a decision. It's not your decision to make for her.'

'It's done, Shirley. It's over.'

Didn't *anyone* understand? He couldn't ask her to stay. He couldn't risk her health. He had to keep her safe even if it meant breaking his own heart. There was no other way.

He looked to the southern sky but the plane had disappeared from view. Rose really was gone from his life.

The significance of his decision sank in.

What had he done?

Rose had accused him of being afraid. He was afraid of falling in love again, but he was even more afraid of losing her. No matter which way you looked at it, Shirley was right—he'd lost her.

But he had no other choice.

CHAPTER TWELVE

IT HAD BEEN thirty days since she'd returned to Adelaide and every morning she woke up and told herself that she'd start making a plan for the rest of her life. Start applying for a job. If she wasn't going to get her happily ever after with Mitch she needed to look for it in other places and other ways. She would have to focus on her career instead. She loved kids, and while she didn't have her own she would put her energy into educating other people's children. It was time to get busy, time to look to her future. It might be different from the one she had hoped for but new possibilities could be exciting and it would help keep her mind off Mitch.

And today really was the day she needed to get moving. Today should have been the end of her three-month stint on Emu Downs. She'd had such dreams and plans. Pie in the sky. She'd been so certain things would work out, that she and Mitch would be able to build something together, but it seemed life, and Mitch, had other ideas.

But she couldn't mourn for ever. She needed to get over him.

She pulled out her laptop. She'd been talking to Ruby about combining her work with some travelling. It was time to get out of here. She needed to get far away. She knew of a couple of people who had studied with her and gone overseas to do some volunteer teaching in the Pacific, Fiji or Vanuatu, she thought. Perhaps that would be a good option, although she had no idea how she would fund that. But it couldn't hurt to look.

She flicked on the kettle and switched on the laptop but just as the kettle boiled there was a knock on the front door.

She opened the door and stood there in shock as thoughts raced through her head, colliding with each other. So many different thoughts she couldn't figure out which ones, if any, she should verbalise.

Mitch and the children stood there. Mitch was staring at her in silence. Was he waiting for her to speak? Expecting her to speak? What on earth did he want her to say? What on earth was he doing here?

The kids had no hesitation. They launched

themselves at her, wrapping their arms around her legs.

'What are you doing here?' Rose asked as the children clung to her.

'We came to see you,' Mitch replied.

'You can't just drop in unannounced whenever you happen to be in the city.' Thank goodness her mother was at work, she thought. She didn't know how she would explain this unexpected turn of events to her. 'Not after making me leave you.' *My heart won't stand it.*

'We didn't just happen to be in the city. We came to see you,' Mitch told her.

'What? Why?'

'May we come in?'

Rose stepped aside.

'I came to apologise,' Mitch said.

Rose sent the children into the kitchen and gave them some muffins she'd baked the day before and a glass of milk each then took Mitch into the lounge where they could talk in private.

'I was wrong,' he said as he paced around the small room. 'I got so caught up in the past that I couldn't see my future. Ever since Cara died I had an ache in my heart. I'd got used to it being there, but it disappears when you're around. For some reason I couldn't see that you were what

I needed until you were gone. We miss you. *I* miss you. I *need* you.'

Rose sat on the sofa. Mitch's pacing was making her nervous. Mitch *being* there was making her nervous. 'I miss you too but I can't see how we're going to resolve things. You aren't going to leave the station and you don't want me there.'

'I do want you there, but you were right. I was afraid.' Mitch sat beside her and picked up her hand. 'I was afraid of losing you but now I've lost you anyway.'

'You didn't lose me,' Rose argued, 'you sent me away.'

'I wanted to keep you safe.'

'And I just wanted you to love me.'

'I do.'

'What?'

'I do love you. I was afraid to love you but I can't help it. I love you. We all love you.'

'Do you mean that?'

'Of course. There's only one thing worse than an old man and that's a foolish old man. And that's what I am. Can you forgive me?' Mitch asked as he got off the couch and down on one knee. 'I love you, Rose, and I want you to be part of our family. I want us to be *your* family. Will you marry me?'

'Marry you?'

'Yes. I want you to come home with me as my wife.'

'Back to the station?'

'Yes.'

'Can I think about it?'

'Think about it? Why? What do you need to think about?'

'Are you going to freak out every time I get a cold?'

'Probably.' He grinned sheepishly. 'But I promise I won't call for the flying doctor every time.'

'And what about if I want to have a baby? Are you going to be okay with a pregnant wife? Are you even prepared to have more children?'

'Can we take things one step at a time?'

'I'm not sure. Are babies a deal-breaker?'

'No. As long as you agree to regular antenatal checks. We can work this out. We *will* work this out. You just have to agree to marry me, to become a family.'

'Do the children know what you're doing here?' she asked. And when Mitch nodded she said, 'Come with me.'

She went back to the kitchen and sat at the table with the children. How she'd missed them, all of them.

'Lila, Jed, Charlie,' she said. 'Your dad has

asked me a very important question but it's one that concerns all of us and I want to know what you think.' She took a deep breath—inhale for four, exhale for eight—in order to gather the courage to ask the children the question, hoping they would give her the answer she so desperately wanted. 'He has asked me to marry him.'

'Did you say yes?' Lila asked, as she bounced out of her chair.

'I wanted to speak to you first,' Rose replied.

'Please, say yes, Rose,' Lila said as she threw her arms around her. 'We miss you.'

'Does that mean you'll come back and live with us?' Charlie asked.

'Yes. it does.' Rose nodded. 'What about you, Jed? What do you think?'

'I miss you too.'

Rose stood up and took Mitch's hands in hers. 'We can't change the past and we can't predict the future. I need you to promise me that you will live in the moment with me. I don't need you to worry about me, I just need you to love me. Is that okay?'

Mitch nodded and she could see tears in his eyes. 'I promise to love you and care for you and make you happy,' he said. 'I don't want to live my life without you. You are my future. You are all I need.'

'And you are everything I want. I love you with all my heart, you and the children.'

'Are you saying yes?'

Rose nodded. 'Yes, I will marry you,' she said as she stepped into his arms.

'Ready?'

Rose looked away from her reflection in the mirror and nodded at her mother.

She straightened her dress. It was her mother's wedding dress, the one she'd worn the only time she'd been a bride, on the day she had married Rose's father. It was a simple lace column dress that had been altered, taking it in at the seams to fit Rose's thinner frame. The dress was a little shorter on Rose but in Queensland's heat that didn't matter. She slipped her feet into her new ballet flats. Lucy had adjusted them also, sewing a narrow band of skin-toned elastic across the centre to help hold them on Rose's feet.

Mitch had lost far more than she had and he was prepared to look to the future. A future with her. She'd even got him to consider returning to medicine. Small steps to begin with. There was the possibility of running a flying doctor clinic on Emu Downs six times a year, and Rose thought that would be a good start. If Mitch could look ahead after the tragedies he had suffered then she could manage without a few toes. It was a small price to pay in exchange for her life. A life she was now going to share with Mitch.

She took a deep breath—inhale for four, exhale for eight. She was ready.

She had something old, something new, something borrowed. And something blue. She put her hand over her heart. Lucy had taken an old photograph of Rose's father and had it printed on blue fabric and stitched it inside the dress, over the left breast, over Rose's heart.

She smiled. 'Ready.'

She picked up her bouquet of golden roses, the only thing Mitch had asked for, and tucked her right arm through her mother's elbow. She held her left hand out to Lila and together the three of them made their way out of the house. They paused on the wide veranda of the homestead and looked out over the garden. It was lush and green after the long-awaited rains and the lawns were filled with wedding guests.

Everything Rose needed was right there. Her sisters, their husbands, Jed, Charlie and, most importantly, Mitch. The family she'd grown up with and the family she was about to become part of all waited for her.

She followed Lila down the wide wooden stairs and across the lawn. At the bottom of the garden the river was flowing again but Rose didn't notice. She only had eyes for Mitch.

He reached out and took her hand as Lucy let go and stepped back with Lila. He winked at her as the minister began the formalities. Their vows were simple.

'I, Rose Lucinda Anderson, take you, Mitchell Paul Reynolds, to be my husband, and you, Lila…' she held her hand out for Lila and the boys to step forward, Lila on her left, Jed on Mitch's right and Charlie in the middle '…Jed and Charlie, to be my family. I promise to love you and care for you all the days of my life.'

'You may kiss your wife.'

Rose's stomach fluttered as Mitch's lips met hers and she knew it was more than excitement. She resisted the temptation to place her hand over her stomach. She was keeping that surprise to herself until she could share it with Mitch when they were alone. She was going to enjoy the day—she didn't plan on having another wedding day and she wanted to make this one special. News that they would be adding to their family could wait.

Today was the start of the rest of her life. The beginning of her future with Mitch.

Today was perfect. She had everything she had ever wanted.